THE
BARN
BURNER

Other Apple Paperbacks for you to enjoy:

Civil War Ghosts
by Daniel Cohen

Freedom's Fire
by J.P. Trent

In the Stone Circle
by Elizabeth Cody Kimmel

The Orphan of Ellis Island
by Elvira Woodruff

The Power of Un
by Nancy Etchemendy

Run Away Home
by Patricia McKissack

THE
BARN
BURNER

PATRICIA WILLIS

AN
APPLE
PAPERBACK

SCHOLASTIC INC.
New York Toronto London Auckland Sydney
Mexico City New Delhi Hong Kong Buenos Aires

No part of this publication may be reproduced in whole or in part,
or stored in a retrieval system, or transmitted in any form or by any
means, electronic, mechanical, photocopying, recording, or otherwise,
without written permission of the publisher. For information regarding
permission, write to Permissions, Houghton Mifflin Company,
215 Park Avenue South, New York, NY 10003.

ISBN 0-439-30528-4

Copyright © 2000 by Patricia Willis
Cover illustration copyright © 2000 by Robert Andrew Parker
All rights reserved. Published by Scholastic, Inc., 557 Broadway,
New York, NY 10012, by arrangement with Houghton Mifflin Company.
SCHOLASTIC, APPLE PAPERBACKS, and associated logos are
trademarks and/or registered trademarks of Scholastic, Inc.

12 11 10 9 8 7 6 5 4 3 2   2 3 4 5 6 7/0

Printed in the U.S.A.   40

First Scholastic printing, May 2002

I am grateful to Lisa Withrow,
for reading and editing this story
with just the right mixture of gentleness
and unflinching honesty.

Thanks also go to Karen Bosyj,
for patiently teaching me
how to live with my computer.

THE
BARN
BURNER

ONE

Ross opened his eyes. It was hard, the first few moments after waking, to remember where he had settled for the night. Light bored through dozens of tiny holes in the tin roof above him, and something rustled in the hay nearby. Now he remembered. In last night's driving rain, he'd taken shelter in a roadside barn.

He sat up. His clothes were still damp and he itched all over. It would be a relief to get out in the sun and dry off. He reached for his knapsack and pulled out the water bottle. Only a few drops remained. Tipping it up, he let the lukewarm water wash away the dryness in his throat. But still he tasted wood smoke. Smoke! He leapt to his feet. He hadn't noticed until that moment that the light inside the barn was murky and blue. Something was burning. Grabbing his knapsack and hat, he scrambled down the hayloft ladder to the main floor.

The night before he'd entered the barn through a wagon doorway, but now he had no idea where it was. Thick smoke obscured everything except the rough planks beneath his feet. The smoke wafted away for a moment, revealing metal stanchions and feed troughs just ahead. That wasn't the way out. Turning aside, he caught a glimpse of flames licking up a wall, but then something cut off his view.

Ross stared at the still, ghostly shape silhouetted against the flames. It looked like a man, though the light was so dim he couldn't be sure. Then the shape moved. It *was* a man, wearing a dark hat that hid his face. When he saw Ross, he spun away.

"Wait!" Ross shouted. "Is there a door?" But the man was already gone.

Ross stepped forward into a furnace blast of heat. Then he saw the torch on the floor, a handful of twisted hay, still smoking. Next to it lay a blue matchbox. Suddenly, a cascade of sparks rained down on him. He grabbed the matchbox and retreated.

For the first time, he became aware of frantic animal noises nearby. He wasn't the only one wanting to escape. He headed toward the sounds. The smoke was thinner here, but a head-high partition blocked his way. Peering over it, he saw two black horses with wild white eyes rearing and snorting, their hooves slamming against the wooden wall. At the far end of the stall was a door that Ross hoped led outside. But he had to get past the horses first. Hesitating only a moment, he pulled himself to the top of the partition, then eased down into the stall. The big animals were terrified and barely took notice of him. They pranced from one side of their stall to the other, tossing their heads and shying away from the mounting flames.

Ross was halfway to the door when one of the horses began backing up. Horses never stepped on a person if they could avoid it, he knew, but those thick, solid hindquarters would crush him against the wall unless he got out of the way. Cringing from the heavy bulk bearing down on him, he felt the leather straps and buckles of a harness on the wall behind him. At the last moment, he clambered up the harness, straining, pulling, clawing his way out of reach.

Boards cracked just below him when the desperate animal smashed into the wall. As soon as the horse danced away, Ross released his hold on the harness straps and dropped to the floor. He ran to the door and flipped up the latch. Then in one violent thrust he flung the door wide open. As he rushed into the clear morning air, the horses stampeded past him. One came so close that its flank brushed against him and knocked him to his knees. He stood up in time to watch the animals disappear around a bend in the road.

Ross took a deep breath. His nose and throat still burned, but the fresh air soon cleared his vision. He gazed at the burning barn, hoping there weren't any more animals inside. Smoke curling through cracks high in the siding told him the fire had reached the haymow. There was no way to stop it now.

Before he could decide which way to go, a man came running around the corner of the barn. This fellow was much taller than the man Ross had seen inside, with broad shoulders and a long neck. The tail of his yellow shirt hung out the sides of his bib overalls. Then Ross's gaze dropped to the club in the man's hand.

The two of them stood staring at each other until the man let out an angry roar. "You! You set my barn on fire. I'll teach you—" He lunged toward Ross with the club raised high over his head.

The man was almost on him before Ross could react. At the last instant, he whirled away into the road, his shoes slipping and sliding in the loose gravel. He ran without looking back. He kept on long after his legs turned to jelly and he began staggering like a newborn colt.

Finally, the pain in his side became unbearable and he had to stop. Even if the man were right behind him, he could go no farther. Bent over, hands on his knees, he sucked air into his tortured lungs. It was several moments before he could even look up. When he did, he saw a dark column of smoke above the trees, marking the location of the burning barn. The man with the club was nowhere in sight.

Ross realized then that he still held the matchbox. He turned it over in his hand. It was pale blue, with silver writing on the top. *Blue Moon Café*. He slid open the miniature drawer. The box was half full of white-tipped matches.

For a moment, Ross considered returning to the barn with the telltale box. But he knew the man who had tried to catch him wouldn't give him a chance to tell his story. Besides, he didn't want to get involved. He thought of the train ride out of Cleveland when he had spied two men stealing a wallet from a sleeping man. They had seen Ross watching them and silently dared him to do something about it. Ross had simply turned his head away. If you wanted to survive on the road, you minded your own business. His business now was to get away from here before anyone else saw him.

He must have gone more than a mile when he rounded a curve in the road and saw a man coming toward him leading two horses. Ross recognized the animals. They were the ones that had run from the burning barn. Evidently, the man was returning them to their owner. If the fellow saw the smoke and questioned him about it, he would just run away—with the horses in tow, the man could never catch him. To Ross's relief, the man passed by with only a nod.

People took little notice of strangers on the roads these days. There were men everywhere, and boys, too, searching for work, following rumors of jobs, walking miles in hopes of earning one day's pay. Times were tough, and people were finding it harder and harder to get by. It seemed to Ross that 1933 was shaping up to be even worse than the year before.

As he walked, his thoughts turned toward home. Everything had started to go wrong when his father lost his job at the lumberyard just before Christmas. People weren't buying lumber anymore. They couldn't afford to build houses or barns. His father had thought Mr. Waverly would take him back when business picked up. But business had gotten worse and worse, until finally Mr. Waverly had closed the lumberyard.

That was when Ross's father began to change. He was angry most of the time, and his anger seemed to center on Ross. One day he whipped Ross with a belt for breaking a window, even though it had been an accident. Ross was punished once because he was too slow bringing water from the well, and another time for tearing his coat. No matter what he did, his father found fault with it.

Ross tried to stay out of his father's way, even skipped meals to avoid him. It wasn't the whippings that kept him away; he had gotten used to them. It was the way the whole family had changed. His brothers and sisters were afraid of their father, and seemed nervous and jumpy even when he wasn't there. And their mother had grown tense and silent.

The night Ross had brought home the live chicken had been the worst time of all. Even now he could hear his father's accusing voice.

"Where'd you get that chicken?"

"From Fred Myers. He—"

"Don't lie to me! You stole it, didn't you?"

"No, I didn't, Papa. Mr. Myers said if I'd help

7

him finish that fence around his wheat field, he'd give me a chicken."

"You've invented a fancy story to cover up your wrongdoing. I've told you all time and time again I won't tolerate any stealing, even if we starve to death."

"I didn't steal it, Papa," Ross pleaded. "I earned it. I didn't tell anyone because I wanted it to be a surprise."

His father had towered over him. "You'll take that chicken back to Fred. Right now."

"I'm telling the truth, Papa. I worked three weeks for that chicken. I won't take it back." Eyes locked on his father, Ross had set the chicken down on the floor.

He saw the backhanded slap coming, but too late to avoid it. The force of it sent him reeling across the kitchen. By the time he had regained his balance, his father was coming at him again.

Suddenly, his mother stepped between them. She faced Ross, hands outstretched, her eyes begging. "Ross, you've got to obey your father." Then she turned to her husband. "Nathan, please . . ." In the middle of her plea, he struck her, a hard-fisted blow on the shoulder that knocked her down on her knees.

Even now Ross could feel the pain from air

trapped in his chest, could still hear the roar that must have been his own raging voice. He had flown at his father, arms swinging, fists pounding in revenge. His father had met his assault head-on, knocked him against the wall, then headed for him again.

Ross's mother jumped to her feet, rushing to get between them. She grabbed Ross and shoved him away. "How dare you strike your father!"

Ross was so stunned he couldn't move. He had only been trying to protect her. She came closer, her eyes flashing fire.

"You're a willful, disrespectful son." She raised her hand, and for a second Ross thought she was going to strike him, too. Instead, she pointed to the door. "Go on. Get out of my sight."

Shocked by her cruel words, Ross looked around the kitchen. Everyone was there: his brothers watching from the doorway, his sister Alice holding Amy tight against her side. There was an awful silence. No one would help him, tell him what to do. Tears stinging his eyes, Ross backed away from them all, and slammed out the door. He stumbled into the cold night, unmindful of anything but his red-hot anger.

Hours passed before he made his way back home. By then his spirit was as dark as the night, but his decision was made. He tiptoed into the still, unlit house and up to his bedroom. Careful not to wake his two brothers, he stuffed some clothes into his knapsack, then, hesitating, went over to the dresser. He reached into the second drawer where he knew his brother Tom kept the money he was saving for a bicycle. Ross felt guilty about stealing it, but he couldn't take the chance of waking his brother to ask for it. Tom probably would refuse and wake the whole household in the process.

He slipped out of the house and walked away without a backward glance. Knowing the quickest way out of town was the railroad, he headed for the tracks. Minutes later, he jumped aboard a slow-moving freight train headed east.

Since that night, he'd had two weeks to reconsider his actions. He didn't think of his leaving as running away. Who could stay where he was not wanted? Now, whenever he thought of home, he renewed the vow he had made to himself that night. He was never going back.

The sun climbed high in the sky as Ross walked along the deserted road. He topped a hill and saw a long valley opening out before him. Maybe he could find someone down there who would let him work for some food.

Nearing a farmhouse, he saw a woman hanging

out washing on a backyard clothesline. "Good morning," he called from a distance, so as not to startle her.

She turned and examined him with open
curiosity, from his stained felt hat down to his dirty
shoes. Ross knew how he must look, his body all
hollows and sharp edges from too little food. His
face and the brown hair straggling from under his
hat had taken on the color of the roads he'd traveled, dusty, rock-gray.

"Where have you come from, young man?"

"I'm on the road, looking for work. Do you
have any jobs that need doing?" he asked.

He could see the rejection in her eyes even
before she spoke. "No. I've got a husband out of
work, and two sons. They do whatever needs to be
done around here."

Ross nodded and hitched his knapsack higher
on his shoulder. Sometimes it took all day to find
a meal, and then it wasn't much, just enough to
dull the sharp edge of his hunger. He was turning
back to the road when the woman's voice stopped
him.

"Wait a minute." She held up a finger, signaling
that Ross should wait there. Then she headed for
her back door. Once she was inside, Ross could
hear voices, hers and a man's rumbling in return.
When she came out the screen door, the man held

the door ajar and called after her, "You don't have to feed every lazy bum that comes by."

The woman ignored him and approached Ross, holding out a sweet potato, plump and hot.

"You ought to go home, young man. Your mother's probably worried about you."

Ross frowned, thinking of his mother's last words. "Get out of my sight." She wasn't worrying one bit about him. He looked at the woman and forced a smile onto his face. "Thank you for the sweet potato."

"I've been wondering about that smoke," she said, pointing over his shoulder. "It looks like it's up on Thompson's Ridge. Did you see anything burning?"

"No," Ross lied. "I didn't come that way."

"There was another barn burned here in Laurel Valley just last week," she said. "They think somebody set it on fire."

Without answering, Ross turned to look at the distant plume of smoke. The barn was probably just a pile of black rubble by this time.

"You be careful where you spend the night, young man," the woman said. "And good luck to you."

"Thanks again for the potato," Ross said, with only a quick backward glance.

Once he was on the main road, he bit into the hot potato. It was the first substantial food he'd had in two days, and it was delicious. In these lean times, most people shared what they had. Most people! Ross grinned, remembering the woman yesterday who had chased him off with her broom.

As he walked, his thoughts kept returning to the burning barn and the ghostly form he had glimpsed inside. The woman who gave him the sweet potato had said another barn had burned the week before. If the man he'd seen was the one setting barns on fire, he ought to be stopped. But I'm the only one who saw him, Ross thought, and if I try to tell anyone, they'll think I'm lying. Besides, Ross had been seen near the fire. The man with the club had gotten a good look at him. So had the man with the horses. Before long, the news would be out that a boy had set the barn on fire.

He had better get away from here as fast as he could. He wished someone would come along in a car so he could hitch a ride. With a little luck, he would be gone from Laurel Valley before anyone could connect him to the burning barn.

TWO

The sun was high in the sky when Ross spied a woman and two children up ahead trying to maneuver a four-wheel cart along the muddy road. Pieces of furniture mixed in with boxes and baskets and cooking pots told Ross that they were moving. The boy, maybe nine or ten years old, pushed against the back of the cart while the woman pulled on a rope attached to the front axle. The little girl, tears streaking her dirty face, pulled at her mother's dress. All three of them were covered with mud.

When Ross drew near, the woman spoke. "Could you help us?"

"Sure," Ross said and tossed his knapsack onto the loaded cart. Once he had found a solid place for his feet, he pushed against the cart, and while the woman pulled, the boy guided the wheels out of the deep rut. The tantalizing aroma of pickles coming from somewhere on the cart made Ross's mouth water.

"Thank you so much," the woman said as Ross retrieved his knapsack. Then she spoke to the girl. "Hannah, I'm sorry about your sore foot, but I just can't carry you. I've got to help with the cart. It's not much farther."

Ross watched them set out, but they had not gone ten feet before they were stuck again. He walked back to the cart. "Maybe I can help you get where you're going."

The woman turned and pointed up the narrow side valley. "We're going to a house up there. It's not far. We'd be much obliged for your help . . . if you have the time."

"I've got time," Ross said, and once again he threw his knapsack onto the cart. The woman didn't know it, but a fellow on the road had no schedule, no appointed times, and no places where he was expect-ed. He did what he wanted, when he wanted. Of course, most of Ross's time was spent looking for food. If he helped them, maybe the woman would give him something to eat. Every day he seemed to be a little thinner. Since leaving home, he'd had to tighten his belt two notches. Well, if he couldn't find any other work, he could hire out as a scarecrow.

"I'll pull," he said to her. She nodded and handed him the rope, then turned to the boy wiping his muddy hands on his trousers. "Jimmy, you and I will push."

Once the cart had been guided to drier ground at the side of the road, Ross and the boy had no trouble keeping it moving. The woman picked up the girl and walked alongside.

"I'm Mary Warfield, and these are my children, Hannah and Jimmy. I have another daughter. She'll be along later." She paused, waiting for Ross to introduce himself.

"I'm Ross Cooper," he said, glancing at the wide-eyed girl clinging to her mother. She wore patched overalls and a blouse speckled with mud.

"You don't live around here, do you?" the woman went on.

"No," Ross said. "I'm looking for work."

"You're not very old to be on the road."

"I'm getting older every day," Ross said with a grin.

The woman smiled back, and the smile seemed to kindle a flame in her brown eyes. It gave Ross a twinge in his chest. His mother had a smile like that, a sunrise kind of smile. He pushed away the painful thought and asked, "You traveled far today?"

"Just a few miles. We were staying with my sister, but we had to leave because they sold their home. A man here in the valley is letting us move into the old house on his property."

She stumbled over a rut and almost dropped Hannah. "I thought there'd be plenty of time to get there and settle in before dark," she said. "But the rain last night made the road so muddy."

Ross nodded, frowning at the mud beneath his feet. His shoes were covered with the brown, sticky ooze. It would take hours to get them cleaned and dried out.

They hadn't gone more than a quarter mile when Mary spoke again. "This is where we turn in." She set Hannah on the ground and strode ahead to open the gate.

A wagon road, looking as if it were seldom used, ran alongside a swollen stream. It was grassy and firm compared with the main road, and the cart moved easily up the valley.

"I haven't seen this house in some time," Mary said. "I hope it's . . ." She didn't finish, but hurried ahead of them, anxious to be the first one to see it.

Ross was pulling hard up a rise when he saw the woman standing as still as a statue. He stared past her at the weathered gray house squatting in a field of winter-deadened weeds. It must have been abandoned for years. The porch floor sagged where a foundation stone had toppled over, and one porch post was missing. The sandstone steps had slipped and slid out of place, making them more an obstacle than an access to the porch. Glass was missing from two front windows.

Ross let the cart roll to a stop. The house wasn't much better than the barn he had slept in last night. He kept staring at it rather than have to look at Mary. She'd implied that the owner was letting her family live here rent-free. It seemed to Ross that if the fellow wanted to be fair about it, he would have paid them to live here.

After several moments of silence, she turned and gazed at Ross, and her voice sounded as hard as a rock. "It's a roof over our heads."

The way she stood there, unyielding and broomstick-straight, made Ross think of an iron-wood tree. They never grew very tall, but they were sturdy and so tough that Ross had once broken an ax trying to chop one down.

He looked back at the shabby house, thinking that the roof probably leaked. Besides that, there were sure to be a couple dozen field mice inside, and at least one snake.

They pulled the cart up to the front of the house, and Ross waited while the rest of them went in to look around. I'll help them unload their things, he thought, then I'll be on my way. The day was fading fast, and he still had to find a place to spend the night. Maybe sleeping under a bridge would be safer than a barn. He didn't want to take the chance of being anywhere near if the barn burner decided to set another fire.

Mary came out on the porch. "There's a back porch that looks safer than this one. Would you boys please bring the cart around there?"

As Ross and Jimmy parked the cart beside the back steps, Mary came and pulled a broom from among her possessions.

"Don't bring anything inside until I sweep out the kitchen."

Ross hadn't heard Jimmy utter a word yet. The boy was thin and gawky but looked as tough as tanned leather. A dark blue cap covered hair so light it was almost white. As they began to lift things from the cart, Ross asked, "How old are you, Jimmy?"

"I'm eleven," Jimmy said. "How old are you?"

"In two years I'll be sixteen," Ross replied.

Jimmy grinned, his teeth gleaming white in his wind-burned face. He spends a lot of time out of doors, Ross guessed, just like me. But at least he has a place to sleep at night.

Afternoon sun slanted across the steps, and long shadows moved back and forth with them as they deposited the family's possessions on the porch. While they were carrying a round kitchen table up the steps, Mary came through the door, sweeping a pile of dusty debris ahead of her. "We'll sleep in the kitchen tonight," she said. "You can put those feather ticks in the far corner by the window. Mr. Barkley won't be delivering the beds until tomorrow."

It was a big kitchen, vacant except for an old cookstove along one wall and an empty woodbox next to it. Ross thought the stove looked usable, even if one leg was missing.

Mary found more things for the boys to do. "Jimmy, will you go gather up some firewood? There may be some dry kindling under the porch. And try to find something to put under the corner of the stove. Ross, I think you're tall enough to fix this stove pipe."

Ross went over and worked the round pipe back into the hole in the chimney. It fit snugly, so there would be no danger of fire. As he watched Mary pull cloth-wrapped dishes out of a bucket, he knew he ought to be going. The sun was low in the west.

"Ross, we'd be pleased to have you stay and eat with us." As if knowing he would accept the invitation, Mary held out the empty bucket. "Could you bring in some water?"

Ross took the bucket. "I'd be obliged for supper. Where do I get the water?"

"There's supposed to be a good spring at the base of the hill. Mr. Barkley promised he would clean it out for me."

Ross headed out the back door in the direction Mary indicated. He could see where weeds had been tramped down; the trail led him straight to the spring. A stream of water rippled out of the hillside and ran into a clear pool. They wouldn't have far to carry their water, Ross thought, as he scooped the bucket full.

On the way back, he noticed smoke coming out of the chimney. The house looked as rundown in back as it did in front, but maybe Mary would be able to make it livable. Ross wondered why her husband was not there to help. He could be at work, but Ross didn't think so. The man surely would have looked over the house and made some repairs, at least fixed the stove, before letting his family move in.

At supper, Mary drew Ross into the casual conversation about gardens and milk cows and the weather. When those subjects had been covered, she began asking him questions.

"Do you have brothers and sisters?"

"Yes, I have two brothers and two sisters. I'm the oldest."

"Does your father have work?"

Mary wasn't prying, Ross knew. She was merely voicing the question on everybody's mind these days. When he told her that his father had not worked for five months, her mind raced ahead.

"I see. You left home so there'd be one less to feed."

Ross did not contradict her. He would have liked to talk to someone about his family, but he couldn't tell these strangers the real reason he had left home.

Mary got up and walked over to the west window. Sun streaming through the dusty glass created a halo around her, and her face was hidden in shadow when she turned back toward the table. "My husband is working out west." There was an uneasy stillness before she went on. "Families ought to be together, especially in hard times."

Ross remained silent, though he wanted to tell her that sometimes it wasn't possible for families to stay together. She would just ask more questions.

The girl, Hannah, leaned toward Ross. "Where do you sleep, Ross Cooper?"

Ross smiled at the girl's blunt question, even as he reminded himself to be careful and not mention the barn. "In a haystack if the weather's clear, and under a bridge if it's raining."

His answer seemed to satisfy Hannah, and she smiled at him. "I'm five years old."

"I would have guessed you were at least seventeen or eighteen," Ross said.

"Oh, no. I won't be that old for a couple more years," Hannah replied.

Mary came and stood behind Hannah's chair. "It's late in the day for you to start out," she said to Ross. "You're welcome to spend the night with us. You can share Jimmy's bed."

Surprised by the quiet invitation, Ross looked across to Jimmy, and the boy grinned and shrugged his shoulders as if to say, "It's all right with me." It didn't take Ross long to decide that sleeping in this cozy kitchen would be a lot better than sleeping out in the weather. He remembered his first days on the road, riding the trains. It hadn't been as easy as he'd imagined. He'd had very little rest because of the coal dust and the cold and the noise of clattering, swaying boxcars. Once in a while he dozed, but it was like trying to sleep on a galloping horse.

"I thank you," he said. "I'll stay."

Mary nodded. "Good. Now we need water for baths."

Ross could have hugged her for those last words. A bath at last! He and Jimmy carried buckets of water from the spring until Mary was satisfied that they had enough.

While the water heated, the boys moved the washtub into the corner behind the stove. Just as Ross was wondering about the lack of privacy, he saw Mary set about screening off the corner. She stood her broom upright in a bucket and wedged firewood around it to hold it erect. Somewhere among her possessions she found a hammer and nail. After pounding the nail into the wall, she brought out an old blanket. With one end secured to the nail in the wall and the other tied to the broom handle, their bathing area was complete and private.

Ross had not bathed since leaving home, and just thinking of the warm, soothing water sent a delicious shiver through him. But he had to wait his turn. Hannah bathed first, then Jimmy, while Ross worked on his muddy shoes. After each bath, a little more hot water was added, so that when it came Ross's turn, the tub was more than half full.

Crouching behind the makeshift curtain, Ross stripped off his clothes, then settled into the water with a soft sigh. He soaked for a long while before he began scrubbing away the grime from his days on the road.

The blanket had sagged in the middle; by stretching his neck, Ross could see out into the room. Though the kitchen was growing darker by the minute, the oil lamp remained unlit. Jimmy sat on the floor scraping mud from his shoes while Mary brushed Hannah's hair. Hannah was humming to herself, a kind of childish lullaby that made Ross smile and want to hum along.

He was about to stand up and dry off when he heard steps outside on the porch. He settled back into the tub, waiting to see who was coming. The corner was as dark as a fruit cellar, so he didn't have to worry about being seen.

As the back door swung open, he raised up just enough to see a girl about his own age step inside. She was carrying a gallon jar of milk, and before Mary could say a word, she started talking.

"I tried to make it before dark, but I couldn't. I had just finished milking Aunt Minnie's cow when Mr. Adams came by with news of another fire. Warner Smith's barn burned ... clear to the ground."

Ross felt a jolt of panic, and his hand slipped off the edge of the tub with a loud splash. Before he could duck, the girl's startled eyes met his across the top of the drooping curtain. For several seconds, Ross couldn't get any air into his lungs. Then he drew in a painful breath and shrank back into the dark corner.

THREE

Ross sank down as low in the water as he could get. It was bad enough having some strange girl catch him in the bathtub, but even worse having her carry on about the barn burning. He held his breath and waited to see if she would say any more about the fire. He heard her whisper, "Who's that?"

"We met him on the way here," Mary replied. "He helped us move in, so I invited him to stay the night. He's on the road."

"What's he doing on the road? He's only a boy."

"He's looking for work, like everybody else. Emily, you were supposed to be home long before this," Mary said. "You know I worry if you're out after dark."

"If it was Jimmy, you wouldn't worry."

"That's different. He's a boy."

"Yeah," Emily said. "And I'm just a girl. If I wore trousers and my name was—"

"We'll not argue about it," Mary interrupted.

As the two of them talked, Ross eased out of the water and dried off, then pulled clean clothes out of his knapsack. Once dressed, he peeped over the blanket. When he saw the girl pick up Hannah and carry her piggyback to her bed, he ducked under the blanket and crossed to the table.

"Ross, this is Emily, my oldest. Emily, come and meet Ross Cooper."

Emily walked over to the table, her cool gaze settling on Ross like a chill night air. She wasn't quite as tall as Ross, but when she folded her arms across her chest and lifted her chin, she seemed to be looking down on him.

Maybe it was her knowing about the burned barn that made it so difficult for Ross to meet that unfriendly stare. He nodded to her and looked away.

Mary broke the uneasy silence. "Would you boys please empty the tub? Emily and I have to bathe."

Ross and Jimmy carried the tub between them while Mary held the back door open. After it had been rinsed and returned to the dark corner, the boys retired to their bed. Ross sank into the feather tick's softness with a sigh. The kitchen was quite dark now, but still Mary didn't light the lamp. Ross drifted off to sleep, only vaguely aware of splashing water and murmuring voices across the room.

A chorus of birdsong woke Ross. Jimmy and the others were still sleeping, but they wouldn't be for long if the birds had their way. Ross crept out of bed and tiptoed to the door.

Just as he stepped out on the porch, the sun edged over the top of the hill. An image rose in his mind of the flat, treeless land in western Ohio where he had grown up. The big sky seemed to press down on the earth. Winds blew unhindered across miles of parched, open fields, lifting up top-soil until it shut out the sun's light. Eastern Ohio was different. Here, softly rounded hills were just coming green. There was plenty of sky, but not too much of it, and the wind was gentle and warm.

Ross went off in search of firewood, hoping it might get him an invitation to breakfast. He returned with an armload of wood just as Jimmy came out on the porch, stretching and yawning. Mary appeared a moment later and smiled at Ross. "You'll stay for breakfast" was all she said before going back inside.

They were soon gathered around the kitchen

table. Breakfast consisted of hot oatmeal with molasses dribbled over it. Ross could have eaten at least two more helpings, but since being on the road he'd learned to be satisfied with any kind and any amount of food.

He recalled his mother fretting over the scarcity of food for the family. She had doled out carefully measured portions to each of them, always making sure to hold back a little for the next meal. He squeezed his eyes shut. No doubt she was relieved to have one less hungry boy at the table. Just then, he looked up and met Emily's probing gaze.

"Mama says you're on the road, looking for work," she said.

"That's right. Me and a lot of other fellas."

"There aren't any jobs around here, are there, Mama?"

Mary shook her head. "No . . . oh, wait. I heard Mr. Barkley say that the Talley Brick Company was opening up again next week. I don't know if they hire boys, but it wouldn't hurt to ask."

Ross had felt a chill in Emily's words, as if she was trying to discourage him from staying. He pretended interest in the job just to annoy her. "Where is the plant?"

"It's on Laurel Creek Road," Mary told him.

"You go down the main road to the crossroads. The schoolhouse is there, so you can't miss the turnoff. Bear right and it's a mile or so to the plant."

"Maybe I'll go over there," Ross said, careful not to look at Emily or her mother. He had no intention of taking a job in this valley, but they didn't need to know it.

"I'm much obliged to you for letting me spend the night," he said. "I'll be on my way now." He rose and crossed the room to get his hat and knapsack. He was almost to the door when Mary's words brought him to a halt.

"Ross, I've been thinking . . . maybe you'd be willing to stay here a few days and help us settle in. There's plenty to be done to make this place livable. I couldn't pay you, but you're welcome to our table and a place to sleep."

Ross looked at Mary's kindly face and longed to say yes. But he couldn't stay. He couldn't even tell her the real reason why he had to go. She'd never believe his story about the burning barn.

"It's mighty nice of you to offer. I'd like to stay and help you, but I . . . I need to be going on. I have to find paying work."

"I understand," Mary said. "I'm grateful for the help you've already given us. Be careful on the road. And if you come this way again, stop by to see us."

Ross looked from Mary to Jimmy to Hannah, and at last his gaze came to rest on Emily. The others appeared sober, almost downcast, as if reluctant to say good-bye, but Emily's face was smooth and indifferent. Ross sensed that beneath the calm exterior she was pleased to see him go.

Jimmy jumped up from the table. "I reckon I'll walk along with you a piece."

As they strolled down the wagon road, Ross tried to draw his thoughts away from the house up the valley. Since he had been on the road, he had learned something about traveling. A journey began with leaving a place. After a while, where you were going became more important than where you had been. But Ross's mind refused to focus on the road ahead. He was still thinking of the ramshackle house up the valley and the kind woman trying to make a home of it.

"I wish I was old enough to go on the road." Jimmy's words broke into Ross's reverie. "I'd get a job and make a lot of money. Papa sends us money . . . when he can."

"There aren't any jobs," came Ross's quick reply. He was sorry the remark sounded so blunt, but it was the truth. "Your father is lucky to have a job, even if it's far away. How long has he been gone?"

"Sixty-four days," Jimmy said without a moment's hesitation.

The careful tabulation told Ross how much Jimmy missed his father. He felt a twinge of envy. He could remember when he had loved his father that way. But no more. That one violent night had destroyed everything between them. And his mother had ordered him to go away. How foolish he had been to think she needed his protection. He didn't regret leaving. It would be just plain stupid to stay where you weren't wanted.

Jimmy stopped and pushed his hands into his pants pockets. "I wish we knew exactly how many days he was going to be gone."

"However many it is," Ross said, "it's one less than it was yesterday."

"I never thought of it that way," Jimmy said. He turned then, ready to head back home. "I hope you find work." As he walked away, he called back over his shoulder, "Good luck."

That's what I need, Ross thought, walking on alone. With a little luck, I can get out of this valley before I run into the man who thinks I burned his barn. With a little luck, I'll find a job, too.

He remembered rolling into Cleveland on a freight train. Everywhere he had gone looking for work there were long lines of men ahead of him.

After a week of shivering nights in dark doorways and dreary days with little food, he had given up on the city. Hungry, his money all gone, he had caught an empty freight heading south.

Dodging the railroad guards had been a constant hazard. Two days ago they had almost caught him. Angry voices just outside the boxcar had alerted him, and he had jumped out into the predawn confusion. Men wielding thick ax handles were swinging at anyone within reach. Ross had ducked a blow meant for his head and taken it on his shoulder instead. In the pandemonium, he had gotten away, running until he could no longer see the train or the enforcers' lanterns. After that, he had made up his mind to walk rather than ride any more trains.

Reaching up, Ross massaged the sore spot on his shoulder. He was lucky. He could have been rounded up with the others. And if they had found out he was only fourteen years old, they would have tried to send him home. But all that was behind him. With a comfortable night's rest and a good breakfast, he was set to face the world again.

The sky was blue, a vibrant, stunning blue that made him think anything was possible. He took off his hat and stuffed it into his knapsack. Lifting his face to the sun, he began to sing the lighthearted tune "Happy Days Are Here Again." Roosevelt had made the song popular during his presidential campaign, and now people sang it in defiance of the hard times.

Ross turned into the main road and hadn't gone far when he heard a vehicle coming up behind him. He tripped over a rut trying to get out of the way, but before he could stick out his thumb, the black Model A Ford had passed him by.

The automobile swayed along in the muddy road for a quarter mile or so, then stopped. Maybe the driver was waiting to give him a lift. Ross sprinted toward it, but as he drew closer, he saw the real reason the car had stopped. It had a flat tire. A gray-haired man in a dark business suit was opening the rumble seat at the rear of the car and pulling out tools.

As soon as he saw Ross, the man smiled and began talking as if they were already acquainted. "This is the second flat I've had since I left home." He winced when he stood erect. "And I've got a sore back to prove it."

"Can I give you a hand?" Ross asked. Once the car was in running order again, the man was bound to offer him a ride.

"Sure can," the man replied.

Ross did not know much about repairing tires,

but under the man's careful direction he removed the wheel and pulled out the inner tube. As they worked, they talked.

"So, you're looking for work, Ross," the man said after introducing himself as Ezra Hamilton. "What about school?"

"My school's already out for the summer," Ross said. There had been two more weeks to go when he left home, but by now the term was finished. It wasn't really important anyway. His school days were over.

"You've done me a good turn today, son," the man said. "Maybe I can steer you to a job. A friend of mine runs the Talley Brick Company. They've been closed over the winter, but they're reopening next week."

"I've heard of that place," Ross said. "But they probably don't hire boys."

"They might," Ezra said. "There's always some kind of job for a boy at a brick plant. If you go over there, ask for Roy Weston. Tell him I sent you."

"Thank you. I will," Ross said. It was just his luck that he would be offered work in a place where he couldn't accept it. People were trying to help him, but all he could do was lie to them. Ever since the barn burning, he had been telling lies.

How many more would he have to tell before he got out of this valley?

As he was pumping up the patched inner tube, he heard another car coming. It pulled alongside and stopped. When he glanced over and saw the silver letters painted on the car door, he bent lower over the pump, his heart hammering in his chest. The sheriff!

A man in a brown uniform appeared around the rear of the car. "Do you need any help?"

"No, we're about finished," Ezra said. "It's the second flat this morning. I wish Henry Ford had built his cars to ride on something besides air."

While Ross worked the wheel onto the axle, he listened to the men talk. The conversation hovered in the air like a thunderstorm, and he felt as if lightning might strike him at any moment. The sheriff surely knew about the barn burning and was probably on the lookout for the boy suspected of setting the fire. Then lightning did strike.

"Is this your boy?" Ross heard the sheriff ask Ezra.

"No," Ezra said. "Ross just happened along and volunteered his help."

Ross could feel the sheriff's eyes burning into his back. "You live around here, Ross?"

Ross swallowed hard and stood up, steeling

himself to face the man and tell another lie. "We just moved into an old house yesterday . . ." He made a vague gesture down the road. It wasn't the whole truth, but it wasn't exactly a lie either. He was not going to tell any more than he had to, and he hoped the sheriff would not decide to investigate his story.

The man studied Ross, seeming to hold him prisoner with his gaze, until Ezra broke the silence.

"Something wrong, Sheriff?"

Those compelling eyes finally set Ross free. "There was a barn burning night before last, and we have reason to believe a boy started it."

"Most likely it was some fellow on the road," Ezra said, "and he got careless with his cigarette."

"Maybe," the sheriff said, "but we would like to talk to the boy just the same. He's wearing a blue striped shirt and a black hat. We're watching the roads. He won't get out of the county." With one last glance at Ross, he walked back to his car and slid into the driver's seat.

Watching the vehicle pull away, Ross began to worry in earnest. The sheriff was suspicious, he could tell. Any second he might turn around and come back to question him about the burning. And if he insisted on looking in Ross's knapsack, he would find the telltale shirt and hat. And the box of matches. Ross's mind whirled, seeking a way out. Even if he caught a ride with Ezra, he wouldn't get past the roadblock that was sure to have been set up.

After Ezra had finished storing his tools in the car, he turned to Ross. "Can I give you a lift?"

Ross watched the sheriff's car grow smaller in the distance, then disappear around a curve in the road. "No, thank you. I . . . I'm not going far," he said. He knew now what he must do. He would go back and accept Mary's offer of room and board. She needed help, but—more important— he needed a place to stay . . . a place to hide.

He thought of the people who had seen him near the burning barn: the barn owner, the man returning the horses. Ross realized that he had left a clear trail, as if he had walked through wet cement. Now the cement was set, and it was too late to obliterate his footprints. All he could do was hide. Then in a few days, when things had quieted down, he could leave. If all went well, he would never see this valley again.

FOUR

As he topped the rise a second time and looked down on the bleak farmhouse, Ross wondered if he had done the right thing by coming back. Maybe Mary was just being polite when she had invited him to stay. He hoped the invitation had been sincere.

By the time he reached the back porch, Jimmy and Hannah were there to greet him. Hannah walked over and looked up at him. "Are you going to be in our family now, Ross Cooper?" Before he could answer her, Mary came through the door.

"I hope you've reconsidered," she said.

Ross was grateful to her for making it so easy. "I just met a man who says I might get a job at the brick plant. I thought I could take you up on your offer of room and board for a few days." If the sheriff had not shown up, Ross never would have returned, but he could not tell them that. He would have to pretend that the job was important to him. Anyway, he could use the money when he went back on the road.

Mary's response settled everything. "We sure can use you. Mr. Barkley brought the rest of the furniture. We were about to set up the beds. You can help."

Emily was staring out the window when Ross and the others walked into the kitchen. Ross knew she must have heard the conversation on the porch, but she made no move to greet him.

They toiled through the morning, cleaning the upstairs rooms, setting up the beds, and carrying the bedding up from the kitchen. For lunch, Mary fried potatoes and onions in a big iron skillet. The potatoes, along with generous slices of bread, fortified them for the long afternoon of work.

Jimmy and Ross were given the task of spading up a plot of ground for a garden. One used the short-handled shovel while the other used the hoe. Sweating and grunting, they labored to turn over the thick sod and break up the clods. Every so often they would trade implements.

Blisters rose in Ross's palms and soon broke

open. He was pulling at the tattered skin when he heard a noise and looked up. Emily stood a few feet away, hands clasped behind her back, her bottom lip caught between her teeth.

"I came to help," she said, her gaze sliding away from Ross to Jimmy.

"This is boys' work," Jimmy said without looking up.

Emily expelled a loud breath. "I can do anything you can do and probably better."

"Girls don't have the muscles for this job."

The grin on Jimmy's face told Ross he was deliberately trying to rile Emily. He succeeded grandly. Her cheeks turned red and her eyes flashed.

"I have just as many muscles as you and a whole lot more brains," she replied.

"Tell her, Ross," Jimmy said. "There are just some things a girl can't do."

Ross hadn't the least intention of telling Emily anything, even before she turned to glare at him. He gladly would have given his hoe to her, but instead he shook his head and went back to work. When several moments passed wthout any more words between Emily and her brother, Ross looked up to see if she had gone away. She was still there, kicking at the upturned earth.

Jimmy reached down at his feet, picked up a

plump pink earthworm, and tossed it at Emily. When it landed on her shoulder, she winced and brushed it off. Then she started toward him, her hands squeezed into tight fists.

Jimmy danced away from her. "Why don't you go inside and wash the dishes or something?" he said to her.

"Why don't you sprout wings and fly away," she growled, then spun around and stalked past Ross without looking at him.

Ross leaned on his hoe and watched her go. Her squared shoulders and lurching stride made him wish Jimmy hadn't been quite so hard on her. She had only wanted to help. Jimmy watched, too, as she slammed through the screen door.

"She's always complaining that she doesn't get to do things. Just because she's a girl, she says."

"My sister Alice says the same thing," Ross replied. "One day she announced that she was going to be a boy. She told us to call her Albert."

"Emily would never pretend to be a boy," Jimmy said. "She doesn't like boys."

Ross knew that already. He had sensed her hostility from the very beginning, even before she knew anything about him. For some reason, she resented him being there.

By the time the boys were called in to supper,

Ross's blisters were raw and sore. They hurt like bee stings when he washed his hands.

After supper, they all wandered out onto the back porch. Mary sat down on the top step, and Hannah dropped on the step below, leaning back against her mother's legs. Jimmy picked up some pebbles and began tossing them at the spade still standing upright in the garden. With both arms wrapped around a porch post, Emily gazed up at the darkening sky.

The day's dying made Ross shrink within himself. In the stillness, his thoughts drifted back home. Were they thinking about him, worrying about him? Did his father and mother regret the argument that had erupted into a vicious battle and sliced the family apart?

Emily's quiet sigh brought Ross back to the dusky porch. Her head was tipped up as if she still scanned the sky, but her eyes were closed. The frown on her face made him wonder if she were thinking of her father.

A sharp crack of thunder startled everyone and brought Jimmy sprinting up on the porch. When the rain came, Mary and Hannah got up and went inside. Jimmy soon followed, leaving Emily and Ross alone in the rainy dusk.

Scooting back from the edge of the porch,

Ross clasped his arms around his bent knees. He liked the sound of the rain. He guessed Emily liked it, too, because she had not moved, even though raindrops pelted her upturned face. The frown was gone. Eyes closed, her face smooth and serene, she idled in the rain like a butterfly basking in the sun.

"I like your valley," Ross said and watched Emily's eyes open and focus on him. "Back home the land is as level as a stovetop, and when the wind blows, there's nothing to stop it but a few trees here and there." He looked past her at the green slopes shaded gray by the rain. "I like these hills."

"How long are you going to stay here?" Emily asked in a voice that was little more than a whisper.

Ross's startled gaze bounced back to meet hers. "Just a few days, I reckon. Your mother wants me to—"

"We don't really need you, you know," Emily interrupted. "Mama is just softhearted . . . and she's partial to boys."

Before Ross could think of a safe response, Emily went on. "I don't understand why people don't stay home." Her gaze fixed on something down the valley; when she spoke again, her voice was low-pitched and far away. "Papa went clear to Colorado, and I don't know if he's ever coming home again." Without waiting for an answer, she hurried past Ross and on into the kitchen.

Emily's words reminded Ross of the men he had met on the road. They were always talking about home and could hardly wait for the day they would return. They had not wanted to leave home, but they'd had no choice. I had no choice either, Ross mused. He sat there listening to the soothing rhythm of the rain on the roof. Home! Somewhere there must be a place he could settle down and call home.

The next morning the boys were spading the last corner of the garden plot when a woman's voice made them both jump.

"Hello, Jimmy. How's my favorite nephew?"

Ross looked around at a middle-aged woman leaning on a cane. On her arm, she carried a wicker basket with green leaves sticking out of it. A wide-brimmed hat shaded her face, but even its shadow could not dim her laughing blue eyes.

"Hi, Aunt Minnie. I'm your *only* nephew," Jimmy said with a grin. As he started toward her, a sharp command brought him to a halt.

"Bring me a handful of that soil," the woman said.

Ross watched Jimmy pick up a big clod of dirt and head for the waiting woman.

"No, not that," she said. "Some of that loose loam."

As Jimmy tossed away the clod and grabbed a handful of the moist earth, he called to Ross. "Come and meet my aunt Minnie. She raises the best garden in Laurel Valley."

When Ross approached them, Jimmy was pouring the soil into his aunt's cupped hands. She rubbed it between her palms, lifted it to her nose to smell it, and then, to Ross's amazement, touched her tongue to it. She closed her eyes as she rolled the grains around in her mouth. Then she spat out the soil and spoke directly to Ross.

"It gives us life, you know."

Both puzzled and fascinated by the woman, Ross watched the dirt filter through her fingers like tiny brown beads.

"Name one thing that doesn't come from the earth," she continued, her piercing gaze prodding Ross to respond.

"Well, I never thought about . . ." His reply faded away.

"We forget that the earth gives us everything—food, fuel, clothes, houses, books." She stopped, and her eyes sparkled as she stretched out a hand to Ross. "I'm happy to make your acquaintance, young man."

Ross took the offered hand, feeling calluses and earth and strength in it. He smiled at the woman. "I'm Ross Cooper."

"I won't keep you from your work," she said. "I brought Mary some tomato plants." As she turned toward the house, she threw a parting comment over her shoulder. "My lettuce is already up, Jimmy."

Jimmy grinned at Ross and shrugged. "Aunt Minnie has her garden in weeks before anyone else. I think along about February she scrapes the snow away and starts planting."

Aunt Minnie stayed for lunch, and the table conversation wound in and out among the valley happenings, until it finally centered on Warner Smith's burned barn.

"Who would do such a thing?" Mary asked, not really expecting an answer.

"Maybe nobody started it on purpose," Jimmy said. "Sometimes green hay catches fire on its own."

"Who's cutting hay this time of year?" Emily countered. Her next remark brought all eyes to her. "I know who did it."

Ross was swallowing a bite of food and almost choked on it. His heart seemed to stop beating as he waited for Emily's next words.

"The fellow who did it is someone who thinks fires are fun, someone who wants to see animals suffer."

Ross swallowed hard, and the food went down, but he didn't raise his eyes. The others would surely be able to see that he knew something about the fire. He hoped they would find something else to talk about, but Aunt Minnie went on about the burning.

"The horses escaped. In fact, they think the person who set the fire must have let them out."

"Did anyone see the man?" Mary asked.

"It was a boy, not a man," Aunt Minnie said. "Warner Smith got a good look at him, too."

Ross couldn't get down another bite. He felt as if he had walked onto a bridge and now it was collapsing beneath him.

"How old was the boy?" Emily asked.

"I don't know," Aunt Minnie replied, "but they said he was wearing a blue striped shirt and a black hat."

The room grew suddenly still. There were vibrations in the air, like a wire humming when it is stretched too tight. Ross finally looked up. Mary was staring at him, frowning. She knew! She remembered that he had been wearing a blue striped shirt and a black hat when he met them on the road.

Heat rose in Ross's face, guilt because he had been there when the barn burned and anger because he was being accused of something he did not do. He could blurt out the whole story and hope they would believe him. But it was a story that needed proof, and he had none. Now even Aunt Minnie was eyeing him. If his knees weren't so weak, he would have jumped up and run out the door.

Aunt Minnie finally broke the silence. "My, it's getting late. I'd better head home." She rose and began to collect the dirty dishes.

"Don't worry about those, Minnie," Mary said. "Emily and I will do them."

In only moments, Aunt Minnie was gone. The kitchen echoed with the clatter of dishes as Mary began to clear the table.

"Jimmy, will you go gather some firewood. Hannah, I'd like you to sweep off the back porch and the steps. Emily, the water bucket is almost empty."

Mary's blunt orders were obeyed at once. The three children scattered to their tasks without a word. Not one of them looked at Ross. Slowly, Ross rose from his chair and faced Mary. This was it, the moment he had been dreading.

Mary startled Ross by coming and placing her hands on his shoulders, holding him as securely as if he were tied. Her gaze burned and chilled him at the same time.

"Were you in Warner Smith's barn that night?"

Ross had to swallow twice before he could get out a sound. "Yes" was all he said.

Mary's breath was like a gust of wind through autumn leaves. "Did you set the fire?"

His answer was barely a whisper. "No."

Moments passed, the only sound the distant swish-swish of Hannah's broom on the porch floor. Ross longed to run out the door, and keep running until he was miles away. But Mary still held him prisoner.

"Then who did it?" she demanded. Ross's shoulders sagged under her hands, but she didn't let go. "Tell me."

They stood there, arm's length apart, while he told the whole story. When he had finished, he waited for her to break the uneasy silence. She had listened intently as if he could be telling the truth, but maybe she was only pretending to believe until she could get away and notify the sheriff.

Finally, Mary's hands dropped from his shoulders. "So you wouldn't recognize the man," she said.

"I don't know. I saw him for only a few seconds.

There was so much smoke, it was like trying to see through muddy water."

"You ran from Warner Smith." Mary's tone was accusing.

"He had a club."

Turning away from him at last, Mary lowered herself into a chair. Then she began to talk, reasoning out loud, making plans, speaking, not expecting an answer. "You can't leave as long as they think the barn burner is a boy. . . . Maybe the fellow will set another fire and they'll catch him. You'll be safe as long as you're here with us."

Ross's throat tightened and his eyes watered as he realized she was making plans to hide him, to protect him. She believed he was innocent.

Just then, Emily stepped inside with a bucket of water. Mary rose from her chair and, crossing to the door, called outside. "Hannah, you and Jimmy come in here." When they were all assembled in the kitchen, Mary retold Ross's story. And without waiting for any response, she went on to explain her plan. "Ross will stay here with us until they find the real barn burner. But you're not to tell anyone he's here."

"It'll be like playing hide-and-seek," Hannah said, smiling over at Ross. He couldn't help but smile back.

"You know that secrets are not to be told," Mary said and eyed each of the children until they nodded back.

Ross noticed that Emily did not look at her mother when she agreed. She was looking at him, and her dark brown eyes were almost black. Ross read in them that she would need proof before she would believe in his innocence.

That night, when everyone was in bed and the old house creaked in the darkness, Ross lay awake wondering if he should sneak off. But the thought of creeping away like a criminal made him angry. The barn burner was bound to be caught sooner or later. Then Ross could go or stay, whichever he wanted, and not have to worry about being arrested for a crime he didn't commit. The night stretched on forever as he argued with himself, too frightened to stay, too stubborn to go.

FIVE

Ross rose early, dressing quietly in the early morning gloom so he wouldn't wake Jimmy. Entering the stove-warmed kitchen, he did not see Mary until she moved. She was standing at the window with her forehead resting against the glass. As she turned, she wiped away tears. Then Ross saw the paper in her hand.

"A neighbor just brought a letter from my husband." She stopped and took a deep breath. "He's broken a leg."

Ross shifted from one foot to the other, wishing he could say something to make her feel better.

"He's all right, but he can't work. And he can't come home. These times are so hard . . ." Mary's voice trembled on the last words.

Ross blurted out the first thing that came into his head. "My brother Tom broke his leg falling out of the hayloft. Nobody was surprised. He's as clumsy as a pig knee-deep in sawdust."

Mary stared at him a moment, then smiled. "I've never seen a pig knee-deep in sawdust."

"I haven't either," Ross said, smiling back. He hoped the tears were gone for good, but seeing Mary's smile fade away, he knew she was still thinking of her husband.

"He's out in Colorado, cutting timber," she said. "He was to be gone only four months. Now it will be a lot longer." She turned and looked out the window again. "We'll just have to be patient until he's able to come home." She went on as if she had forgotten Ross was there. "He won't be able to send any more money, but we'll get by."

There was the same ironwood strength in her voice that Ross had heard once before. It made him feel better.

Mary finally remembered him. "There's warm water on the stove to wash up. I'll fry you a piece of bread dough for your breakfast."

Ross breathed in the mouth-watering aroma of baking bread. Bread pans crowded the back of the stove, with white dough billowing over the edges like wind-carved snowdrifts. How was Mary going to buy bread flour if her husband couldn't send her money?

While he ate, Ross thought about how hard it would be for Mary to take care of her family without any money. As far as he could tell, she had no way of earning any. But I have a way, Ross thought, if Ezra Hamilton was right about the brick plant. Working just one day a week, he could make enough to buy flour. He finished the last of his food, then told Mary what he intended to do.

"I was thinking maybe I'd walk over to the brick plant and see about a job."

"But I thought we agreed you should stay out of people's way," Mary said. "Until they catch the barn burner."

"Warner Smith and the man who brought back the horses were the only ones who saw me there. And they're on the other side of the valley."

Mary pondered what he had said. "I guess you're right, Ross. If you just went to the plant and back, there wouldn't be much risk of running into those two men."

"And if I got a job, I could pay for my room and board."

Mary seemed to understand what he was trying to do. "That isn't necessary, Ross. You're earning your keep with the work you do."

"But you'll need money," he blurted out, then tried to cover up his hasty remark. "I hope they hire boys. There are a lot of men out of work."

Mary smiled at him. "Just remind them that they don't have to pay a boy as much as they do a man. Though I have no doubt that you can do a man's work."

Later, as he was about to go out the door, he saw Mary coming with a brown paper package.

"If they put you to work today, you'll need something to eat," she said.

He hoped they would put him to work. Even though Mary didn't want him to pay for his room and board, Ross felt as though it was his responsibility. It took a lot of food to feed five people.

All the way down the main road, he worried about meeting the sheriff, but once he reached the crossroads and turned into the side road, he began to relax. It wasn't long before he rounded a curve and saw a big wooden building looming on the right. A crushed-brick road led into the plant yard.

Ross headed for the large building and pushed open the door marked Office. Two men were leaning over a desk, studying a map.

"Excuse me," Ross said. "I'm looking for Mr. Weston."

"I'm Weston," one of the men said. "What can I do for you?"

"Ezra Hamilton told me you might give me a job."

The man lifted his hat and ran a hand through his gray hair. "I talked to Ezra yesterday, and he said he was sending me a boy who's a good worker. Are you that boy?"

"I reckon so. I mean, I'm Ross Cooper and I can work."

"Have you worked in a clay plant before?"

"No, sir, but I can learn. I'd be much obliged for the chance to learn."

"There are a lot of men looking for jobs so they can feed their families," Weston said.

Ross thought of Mary's earlier comment. "I know, but you won't have to pay me as much as you would a man."

"Well, that's true," Weston said, grinning at the other man. "Where do you live, Ross?"

For only a second, Ross hesitated, then went on to tell his half truth. "About two miles from here." As the man studied him without speaking, Ross added, "It's not far, and I'll get to work on time."

The man held out his hand. "I'll take a chance on you, Ross, since you come so highly recommended. But it'll be only two days a week. Can you start today?"

"Yes, sir," Ross said, grinning, then winced at the man's painful handshake.

"We'll pay you fifteen cents an hour, and we start at six-thirty in the morning. Dan, take him out and put him to work with Calvin on the bee-hives."

The other man slid a pencil behind his ear and smiled at Ross. "Come along, son. Did you bring gloves?"

Ross shook his head, still puzzling over Mr. Weston's last remark. What in the world did bees have to do with making bricks?

"Maybe I can find you a pair," Dan was saying. "Bricks are rough on hands, especially the first day or so. We'll start you on a shovel today."

Ross almost groaned aloud. He'd done too much shoveling yesterday and had the blisters to prove it.

Dan led the way toward a row of round brick buildings that looked like giant bowls turned upside down. Beside each one rose a slender brick smokestack. A man was working next to one of the buildings, shoveling ashes out of a pit built into the wall.

When they drew near, Dan spoke to the man.

"Calvin, this is Ross Cooper. He's going to help you today."

"That's just the kind of help I need," the man said, eyeing Ross. "Some puny fella that can't do half a day's work."

"Just show him what to do, Calvin, and give him a chance to prove himself. Maybe he'll surprise you." Dan turned to Ross. "I'll look for some gloves." Then he patted Ross on the shoulder and walked away.

"You take over here, boy, while I rest," Calvin said. He pulled off his hat and wiped the inside band with a ragged red handkerchief.

Ross took the shovel and went to work. Despite the wooden handle rubbing his already sore hands, he kept at it. He would show the man he wasn't puny.

"This your first job?" Calvin asked.

There was something in the man's tone that made Ross's spirit rise in self-defense. "No," he replied, "but it's the first one at a brick plant."

"We'll see how long you last."

Ross finished filling the wheelbarrow, then, heading where Calvin pointed, dumped the load on the ash heap by the road. When he returned, Calvin motioned him toward another fire pit farther around the wall.

After several minutes of work, Ross stopped

and leaned on the shovel. "Mr. Weston said I'd be working on the beehives."

"Yeah, well, you're working, aren't you?"

Ross was confused. He hadn't seen any beehives. "But where are the bees?"

"Bees?" Calvin stared at him. "Bees?" Then he gave a loud snort. "You thought . . . you thought he meant real beehives." He broke out laughing, slapping his hand on his leg. He laughed and laughed while Ross stood there red-faced, knowing he had made some dumb mistake but not sure what it was.

"How can you live around here and not know about beehives?" Calvin said at last. "Your education's been badly neglected." He stepped over and laid a hand on the brick wall next to Ross.

"This is a beehive . . . a beehive kiln. It's a big oven. The bricks are stacked inside; then they're baked. Just like your mama's bread."

Ross felt his face flush again. He sure had a lot to learn about making bricks. But he couldn't help wishing he had a different teacher, someone who did not make him feel half the size of an ant. Since Calvin already thought he was stupid, he might as well get the rest of his questions answered.

"Why are they called beehives?" he asked.

Before answering, Calvin pulled a pack of

tobacco out of his shirt pocket and began rolling a cigarette. "When they first started building these kilns, people thought they looked like beehives. So that's what they called 'em."

"And these pits around the wall are where the fires are built?" Ross asked, beginning to understand the brick-baking process at last.

"Now you're getting the picture," Calvin said. "That's my job, keeping the fires going. And cleaning out the ashes afterwards," he added. He struck a match to light his cigarette, and it was then that Ross saw the matchbox. Pale blue, with *Blue Moon Café* printed in silver on top.

Ross turned away, his heart thumping. Was Calvin the man he had seen in the burning barn? He tried to recall the image of the shadowy figure slipping off through the smoke. Calvin seemed to be about the same size. If only he had gotten a look at the man's face. Ezra Hamilton was probably right when he told the sheriff the barn burner was just passing through. The man must be miles from Laurel Valley by now. But as Ross continued working, he gazed now and then at Calvin, wondering.

When they had finished clearing out all the fire pits on that beehive, they went on to the next in line. By the time the lunch whistle blew, Ross was tired and sweaty and hungry. He picked up his lunch and moved toward the group of men congregating under an oak tree near the railroad siding. A man with coal-black hair and a mustache to match motioned for Ross to sit next to him. "You must be new," he said.

"I just started today. I'm Ross Cooper."

"I'm Johnny Peale. I haven't seen you around. Where do you live, Ross?"

"About two miles from here," Ross replied, hoping the man would not ask any questions he didn't want to answer.

"Where, exactly?" the man persisted.

"The old Barkley farm."

"Nobody was living there last I heard."

"We just moved in on the weekend," Ross said. "Where do you live?"

"Greenwood Park," Johnny said, assuming Ross would know where it was. "Guess you know about the shortcut."

"What shortcut?"

"You see that road over there, running along-side the hill?" The man pointed to the gravel road that climbed the slope and disappeared into the trees. "That's Sweet Spring Road. It'll take you by the back side of the Barkley place. Probably cut three-quarters of a mile off your walk."

"Thanks for telling me," Ross said. "I won't have to get up so early in the morning." More important, he wouldn't have to walk the main road and risk meeting the sheriff.

"You been working without gloves?" Johnny asked, leaning over to look closer at Ross's hands. "No surprise you've got blisters already."

"I had them before I came here," Ross told him. "From spading a garden yesterday."

"Handling bricks is ten times worse than spading," Johnny said. "It's like rubbing all day against sandpaper."

"I haven't handled any bricks yet," Ross admitted. "I've been shoveling ashes."

Just then, a tattered pair of gloves fell on the ground next to him. "There's not much left of them," Dan said, "but maybe they'll help a little. Your mama can mend them."

Ross slipped on the right glove. There were holes in all the fingers, but the palm was still intact. He looked up at Dan and grinned. "Yes, sir. They'll cover some of the blisters. Thanks a lot."

Ross was grateful for the rest and the good lunch Mary had packed. There was a piece of fried dough, two slices of bacon, and two big strawberries rolled in a lettuce leaf. He couldn't help but notice Johnny's lunch, one slice of bread with something white spread on it, and a raw, wrinkled turnip. How lucky I am, Ross thought, that Mary took me in. There are lots of people going hungry day after day. The noontime conversation among the workers was about this very subject.

"Roosevelt is going to straighten things out," one man said. "But he has to have time to do it."

"The hell with him," another man grumbled. "He's just another rich man who's never been hungry a day in his life."

"Or watched his family go hungry," Johnny spoke up. "If he'd make the farmers share some of what they have, all of us could eat."

"We spaded up our front yard this spring and put in a garden," a man piped up.

"That's all right for you," Johnny said, "but I don't have any yard to spade up."

Listening to the talk, Ross considered himself lucky that he had no one to take care of except himself. But he knew what it felt like to be hungry. He had missed a lot of meals on the road.

By midafternoon, Ross and Calvin had finished removing the ashes from all eight kilns. They returned to the first beehive, where two men were taking bricks from a flatbed cart by the door and stacking them inside. Layer by layer, their neat pile rose toward the domed roof. The bricks looked gritty and soft, and when Ross touched one, his finger left a slight indentation in the clay.

"We're about finished, Calvin," one of the men said. "You can start your fires anytime." He winked at Ross. "You stick with Calvin and you'll learn the art of fire making."

The casual remark made Ross turn to take a closer look at Calvin. Barn burners were good at building fires, too. He shook his head and followed Calvin outside. He couldn't go around thinking every man he met was the barn burner.

After laying a pyramid of wood chips and small split logs in one of the fire pits, Calvin brushed a match to life against his trousers. The dry wood caught fire at once.

"Now, when it burns down a little," he said, "you can start shoveling in coal." He pointed to the black mounds of coal that had been dumped close by the beehive wall.

Gloves did help a little, but by quitting time, Ross's hands were throbbing. He was glad he didn't have to work the next day. The blisters would have time to heal a little—unless Mary had more shoveling for him to do. He hoped she knew how to mend gloves.

As he was walking across the plant yard on his way home, he saw Johnny Peale and Mr. Weston near the office door. They were talking in loud, angry voices.

"You stacked those bricks, didn't you?" Mr. Weston was saying.

"Yes, I stacked 'em, but you can't blame me—"

"If they'd been stacked right, they wouldn't have collapsed. We not only lost the bricks, we burned up a lot of coal for nothing."

Johnny pulled off his hat and slapped it against his leg, then stomped off a few steps. Suddenly, he turned, pointing the hat at Mr. Weston.

Ross hurried on toward the plant gate. He didn't like arguments. From his own experience, he knew that nothing was settled by arguing, and sometimes the arguments turned into fights. He was glad when he could no longer hear the two men.

SIX

Overhanging trees made a cool, shady tunnel over the gravel road Johnny Peale had pointed out. No houses, no cars, not even a cow in the roadside pasture. There wasn't much chance of meeting the sheriff in such a forsaken spot. Ross walked along, wishing he could follow the deserted road until he came to a place where people knew nothing about burning barns.

He had walked for several minutes when he heard a man's voice. It seemed to come from up ahead, around the bend. The voice rose and fell, first coaxing, then threatening, then screeching words Ross couldn't make out. He hurried toward the noise and, moments later, saw a man wrestling with a brown and white goat. He held the animal by the horns and was trying to drag it through a partially opened gate. More goats milled around, some in the road, some on the pasture side of the fence. While the man was pulling the goat through the gate, two others walked out into the road.

The man, not much taller than the gatepost, clapped his hands at them and hollered, "You stubborn critters! You're going to be sorry. I'll sell every last one of you to the glue factory." Then he looked up and saw Ross. He grinned, and Ross noticed that one of his front teeth was missing.

"Do you need some help?" Ross asked.

"Yes, sirree. I'm trying to get these dumb animals back in the pasture, but they're not cooperating one bit. If you can help round them up, I'll be as happy as a pig in a mud hole."

Ross grabbed a goat by the neck, but the wiry animal was so strong it jerked him off his feet. He managed to hold on and, scrambling to his feet, pulled the animal through the gate. In spite of the goats' balking and bleating, they were all herded into the pasture at last. The man quickly latched the gate behind them, then turned to study Ross.

"I don't know you, but I reckon I know your folks 'cause I've lived in Laurel Valley all my life. What's your name?"

"I'm Ross Cooper. I'm staying with Mary Warfield. She just moved—"

"Into the old Barkley place. I saw her a couple of weeks ago in town and she said she was moving. She never mentioned you. You must be on the road."

"That's right," Ross said. "But Mrs. Warfield needed help moving. She asked me to stay on and help her get settled." It felt good to tell the truth about himself. "I just got a job today at the brick plant."

"Worked there myself when I was younger. All my family did. Now my brother Sidney sells Mr. Ford's cars, and my other brother farms. By the way, I'm Summer Smith." The man extended a hand and Ross shook it. "My mother named me Winter 'cause that was her maiden name, but someone called me Summer and it stuck. Everybody loves a joke." He grinned that tooth-missing grin again, and Ross couldn't help but grin back.

"Since you're going right by my house, you can stop in and see my new litter of puppies."

They fell into step, the man talking as if Ross were an old friend. The house was not more than ten feet from the road, a small, square box of a house, gray with age, like its owner. The place seemed just right for the little man.

A vine climbed one end of the porch and sheltered the box of puppies. They peered out of the shadows, whimpering. The mother dog, all black except for a white throat and white feet, stood in front of the box, eyeing Ross, ears laid flat against her head.

Ross tried to count the puppies, but every time he arrived at a number, another one would appear. He leaned against a porch post and waited for them to venture out. One by one, they inched into view until there were seven.

"You working every day?" Summer asked.

"No. Just two days a week."

"Then I reckon you might be interested in a trade—some work for some food."

"What do you mean?" Ross asked.

"I need help mending the fence so I can keep those pesky goats in the pasture. I could give you some eggs for your help." The man looked at Ross and waited.

Ross thought of Mary trying to feed her family without money to buy anything. "I guess I can do that," he said. "I don't go back to the brick plant until Thursday."

"Good. Reckon you could come tomorrow?"

"Sure. Will you be able to keep the goats in until then?"

"I've propped up the posts that need to be reset. They'll hold a day or so. Don't come early 'cause I don't talk in the mornings. Come in the afternoon."

With their plans set, Ross headed home. Further down Sweet Spring Road, a narrow green valley opened on his right. Only one house was visible, and it was the Barkley place. There was no mistaking the weathered-gray siding and the gray slate roof. Johnny Peale's shortcut had worked out just fine.

Around the supper table, conversation centered on Ross's job.

"What kind of work did you do?" Jimmy questioned.

"Did you get paid?" Hannah asked.

"Did you get to go into a beehive?" Jimmy continued.

Mary finally interrupted. "Children, please! Give Ross a chance to answer at least one of your questions."

"What did you do all day?" Jimmy asked.

Ross turned his hands so that Jimmy could see the broken blisters. There were blisters on his fingers as well as his palms now. "I shoveled ashes and coal."

"Let me see," Mary said, taking Ross's hands in her own.

"A man gave me a pair of gloves," Ross told her, "but they have a lot of holes in them."

"Where are they? Maybe they can be mended."

Ross pulled them out of his back pocket. After a quick inspection, Mary laid them on the floor beside her chair. "They can be patched. But right now, we have to do something about those hands. Emily, bring me that can of salve off the shelf." When Emily came with the salve, Mary stood up. "Spread some on those blisters, Emily, while I go get some clean cloths."

Emily hesitated a moment before sinking down into her mother's chair. As she worked to remove the can lid, her hair fell forward, hiding most of her face. She seemed engrossed in her task, her bottom lip caught between her teeth. But her cheeks were telltale red. She didn't want to do this, Ross knew, but she couldn't refuse without giving her mother a reason. Ross wondered what that reason really was.

He laid his hands on his knees, palms up, holding perfectly still as she began spreading the salve. At least she was being gentle, he thought, trying not to smile. With Mary upstairs and Hannah and Jimmy out on the porch, the room was as quiet an empty church.

"Thank you, Doctor," he said, hoping to m her smile.

Emily's eyes flashed up at him, then back to his hands. "It's women's work."

"You're very good at it. Doctoring, I mean."

"You don't have to lie just to try and make me feel good."

"I don't lie," Ross declared, and then blushed, recalling all the lies he had told in the past few days to avoid being arrested.

"You don't?" Emily looked at him with a level gaze that made him feel like a fly caught in a spider's web. Before he could speak, she went on. "Did you really see the barn burner?"

"I don't know for sure. But I found a box of matches in the exact spot where he'd been standing. And he ran when he saw me."

Emily replaced the lid on the salve and stood up. "I guess we'll just have to wait and see if they catch this man."

At that moment, Mary came into the kitchen. "We'll wrap up your hands tonight, Ross, to keep the salve on them," she said. "They should be better by morning."

Ross wasn't as concerned about his hands as he about Emily. She might convince herself that as the barn burner and think it was her duty to him in.

Later that night with Jimmy snoring softly beside him, Ross lay awake pondering what he could do about Emily. Maybe if he talked to her, he could persuade her of his innocence, or at least create some doubt in her mind. He had the strange feeling that the barn burner was still around and would strike again. If he did, then Emily would know that it was someone else burning barns in the valley.

Ross remembered one night on a train, listening to some men talking about people who set fires. They said each barn burner had his own reasons for torching a building. One remarked that some people just liked to watch things burn. Ross wondered about the man he had seen. Why had he decided to burn that particular barn? And why did I have to pick that barn to sleep in?

He was relieved that Mary and the others knew about his being in the barn. There was nothing else to hide. Except his reason for leaving home. But they would never need to know about that. Emily! She was the problem. Whenever she was near, he felt as if a swarm of bees was circling around him, not stinging but about to strike at any second. He went to sleep with bees and bee-hives and burning barns whirling in his brain.

SEVEN

Ross and Jimmy arose early the next morning, but not as early as Mary, who had already cooked a kettle of oatmeal.

"Let me see your hands," she said. Ross stood before her and let her unwind the bandages. The blisters were still visible, but the soreness was almost gone.

"They look much better," she said. "Do you think they're well enough for you to help Jimmy gather some firewood after breakfast?" When Ross nodded, she reached down into a vacant chair and brought up Ross's gloves. Every hole had been neatly patched. "These will give you some protection."

She must have been up at first light working

on them, Ross thought. "Thank you," he said, and once again Mary's warm smile made him think of his mother. She could sew beautifully, but most of her sewing was repair work, mending tears, darning, patching holes. He pushed the image of his mother back into a dark corner of his mind. He wasn't going to waste time thinking about home.

After they had eaten, Ross and Jimmy headed for the woods beyond the stream. There was plenty of dead wood on the ground, and they soon collected all they could carry. They had just crossed back over the stream when Jimmy stopped and peered into a dense tangle of bushes.

"There's something in there," he said, dropping his firewood and pushing into the thick brambles. Ross put down his load of wood and followed. What they found was a little rundown building that was almost covered with blackberry bushes.

"It's a chicken coop," Jimmy announced with a big grin. "Just what Mama's been wanting."

"But you don't have any chickens," Ross reminded him.

"All it takes is one good setting hen and you're in business."

The door hung on one hinge, but they were

able to force it open enough to squeeze inside. Light coming through a hole in the roof illuminated several box nests along one wall.

"It needs some work," Jimmy said, "but we can fix it up." He looked over at Ross, his eyes sparkling. "I have an idea. We won't tell Mama about it until it's ready. We'll make it her birthday present. Won't she be surprised?"

"Won't who be surprised?" It was Emily, leaning through the doorway.

"Eavesdropper!" Jimmy said. "Well, as long as you're here, you might as well know. We found this chicken coop, and we're going to fix it up for Mama. For her birthday. You have to promise you won't tell."

"Okay, okay. I can keep a secret. And I wasn't eavesdropping. Mama sent me to find you. She wants you to go to Aunt Minnie's and get her garden cultivator."

Jimmy pushed past his sister, pausing to call back over his shoulder. "Remember. It's a secret." Then he was gone.

After glancing at Ross, Emily turned quickly away. But Ross wasn't about to let her escape. This was his chance to talk to her about the barn burning. He caught up with her and laid a hand on her shoulder.

She spun around, her eyes wide, then narrowing as she looked down at his hand.

Ross let it fall away. "Emily, I know what you've been thinking, but I did not burn down Warner Smith's barn."

"But you were there."

"Yes, I was there. But when I woke up, the barn was already full of smoke."

"Why should I believe you?" She plucked a leaf from a nearby bush and rolled it around one finger. "Mama believes you, but she's not thinking clearly right now, with Papa gone, and her not knowing if—not knowing when he'll be back."

Ross noticed her quick correction. She and her mother must both be worrying that Mr. Warfield might never come back. From the things he had heard on the road, Ross was sure Emily's father would return, once his broken leg healed.

"He'll be back," Ross said, wanting to reassure her.

"You don't know anything about it . . . about him."

"I've been on the road, and I've seen lots of men who've been away from their families for months. All they talk about is going home."

Emily studied him for a moment. "That's what you should do. Go home."

"I can't," Ross blurted out without thinking.

Emily looked surprised. "Why not?"

Ross's gaze rested on her, but he was seeing his mother's face when she had spoken those last, devastating words. "Get out of my sight." They still had the power to hurt him. Sometimes the pain was like an iron clamp tightening around his chest. Ross shook his head, not trusting himself to answer Emily.

"Why don't you just leave?" she said. "That way, we won't have to worry about protecting someone who—"

"I'm not leaving," Ross broke in. "Not until they find the real barn burner." And, he added to himself, if the people in the valley can't find the man who's setting the fires, I'll do it for them. While everyone else was looking for a boy, he would be looking for the man he had seen in Warner Smith's barn.

Ross leaned over until his face was only inches from Emily's. "I'm not leaving," he said again. "And if you tell the sheriff and he puts me in jail, the real barn burner will still be running loose. And you will be responsible for the barns he burns down."

A shadow of uncertainty flitted across Emily's face. Without saying another word, she turned and plunged into the briar patch.

Ross ground his teeth together. If it weren't for Emily, he would feel safe here. The old farmhouse was far enough off the main road that no one could see it. And Mary didn't have many visitors. It was true he took a chance working at the brick plant, but he had to risk it to help Mary. With a little luck, he might be able to stay here until her husband came home. If Emily didn't do something spiteful, that is. He felt as though he were teetering on the edge of a cliff, and at any moment Emily might push him over.

At lunch, Ross told Mary about meeting Summer Smith and about his promise to help the little man mend the pasture fence.

"Summer Smith's crazy," Hannah said, as if it was something everybody knew already.

"Hannah! You'll not say such things," Mary scolded.

"But he has a pet lizard that sleeps in his kitchen cupboard, and he keeps a coffin full of—"

"Enough!" Mary almost shouted. "If I hear any more comments like that from you, young lady, I will wash out your mouth with soap."

Emily took up the argument. "But everyone in Laurel Valley knows he burned down his own house."

Flashing a warning glance in Emily's direction, Mary turned to Ross. "People said he set the place on fire, but people love to gossip." She looked again at Emily, frowning. "Even if he did burn down the house, it's no one else's affair."

Ross recalled the Summer Smith of the day before, with his friendly, missing-tooth grin. It was hard to imagine the little man deliberately burning down a house. Whatever Summer might have done in the past really didn't matter anyway, Ross thought. He liked the man.

It was midafternoon when Ross approached Summer Smith's house. A team of horses stood hitched to a wagon at the edge of the road, switching their tails and stamping their feet to chase away the flies. They looked familiar, but then horses all looked alike to Ross. On the porch, the timid puppies scampered back into their box while their mother kept a wary eye on Ross. There was no sign of Summer, but Ross heard voices out behind the house. He strolled in that direction.

Summer was standing by the back steps talking to a man who towered at least a foot above him. As Ross's gaze rose to the tall man's face, he gasped and ducked back out of sight. It was the man who had chased him away from the burning barn. What was Warner Smith doing here?

It did not take Ross long to make the connection. Warner Smith must be Summer's brother, and those horses by the road were the ones Ross had let out of the barn.

Spinning first in one direction, then another, Ross searched for cover. The men hadn't seen him yet. He had to hide before they came around the house. But where? There wasn't another building in sight, no cellar steps, not even any shrubs. A twisted old tree beside the front porch was his only hope.

He ran and grabbed for the lowest limb, but miscalculated and fell to the ground. He could hear the men coming. Springing to his feet, he hurled himself at the limb again and this time held on. With his stomach over the limb, he pulled up his legs and clambered high into the thick foliage.

His gasping breaths sounded like the panting of a train engine. Leaning against the rough tree trunk, he coaxed his breathing to slow and his body to be still. Then he gazed down and waited.

The men came nearer and paused beneath the tree, talking. Ross looked down on them, his heart pounding as loud as a blacksmith's hammer. They surely could hear it.

The mother dog had come off the porch and

now stood leaning against Summer's leg. Then, as if she suddenly remembered Ross's frantic getaway, she gazed up at him. "Don't," Ross silently pleaded and turned his head, closing his eyes, hoping the dog would not bark at him. When he looked down again, Summer was stooped beside the dog, an arm spread over her glossy black shoulders.

"Then you think the fellow is still in the valley," Summer was saying.

"Yes. I think he's biding his time until things settle down. When the sheriff gets tired of looking for him, he'll leave. Or else he'll burn down another barn. I just wish I could get my hands on him."

"It's best to let the law handle it," Summer said.

"If you'd lost your barn, you might think differently about it. Well, don't forget Sunday. We'll eat about one."

"I'll be there," Summer said.

Warner Smith moved out of sight. A moment later Ross heard the slap of leather and the jingle of horse harness. Summer stood gazing down the road as the sounds of the rolling wagon gradually faded away.

Ross didn't know what to do. Sooner or later

he would have to get down out of the tree. Maybe Summer would go in the house. Then he could climb down and pretend he had just arrived.

Ross almost lost his grip when Summer looked up into the tree and said, "You can come down now."

EIGHT

Ross let the air ease out of his lungs, then slowly began working his way to the ground. Still kneeling by the dog, Summer looked up at him, a question in his eyes.

There wasn't any use in trying to explain, Ross thought. He would just go back to Mary's house, pick up his knapsack, and leave. By the time Summer got to the sheriff's office he would be gone, and he would make sure that they didn't find him.

"I'd better be going." He kept some distance between himself and Summer, in case the man tried to grab him and hold him there.

"I think you should tell me why you were up my tree."

Ross lifted his hands, palms up, then let them fall again without speaking.

"It has to do with my brother's barn, doesn't it?" When Ross did not answer, Summer went on. "The fence still needs fixing, and I hold you to your promise. But first, I want you to tell me what happened. Let's go sit down. Come along, Lady," he told the dog and turned toward the porch without waiting to see if Ross would follow.

Ross lagged behind, his stomach churning. He would have to tell his story—not that Summer would believe it. And he guessed he could still help with the fence. Mary needed those eggs. As long as he kept Summer in sight, the man couldn't go off and tell anyone about him.

Summer dropped into the solitary chair, and Ross, his back against a porch post, told of the rainy night and the early-morning fire.

"That's quite a story," Summer said when he had finished.

Ross shrugged, an apologetic smile flitting across his face. The story sounded suspicious even to him. It was the kind of tale a person would spin in order to avoid blame and punishment. There was no way anybody in his right mind was going to believe it.

"I believe it," Summer said, as if responding to Ross's thoughts.

For a moment Ross froze; then his shoulders sagged and tears filled his eyes. He didn't trust his voice to speak, even if he could have found the right words to tell Summer what it meant to have the man believe him.

Summer rose to his feet, dismissing the whole subject. "We'd better get busy on that fence before the goats decide to go for another walk. The tools are around back."

Ross followed the little man, his mind a whirlpool of questions. Why did Summer believe his story? Wasn't he going to ask him anything about it? After all, it was his brother's barn that had burned. There was one question Ross was dying to ask. Why hadn't Summer told his brother that Ross was up in the tree? Maybe it was just another one of the man's strange ways that made people call him crazy. Whatever the reason, he had saved Ross . . . for the moment.

But the danger was still there. If Ross ever came face to face with Warner Smith, the man certainly would want revenge. Other people in the valley would feel the same way, people whose barns had been burned. Then Ross had the most ridiculous thought. The safest place for him now just might be the sheriff's office.

Summer handed Ross the shovel, then swung

the roll of woven wire up on his shoulder. "There are six posts that need resetting, and we'll have to tack on some extra wire. I hope you ate a hefty lunch."

Ross nodded, then dared to ask his burning question. "Why didn't you tell your brother I was up in the tree?"

"I reckoned you must have a pretty good reason for hiding."

"Saving my life seemed like a good enough reason to me," Ross said with a grin.

"My brother is more bark than bite" was all Summer said.

Remembering the look on Warner Smith's face the morning of the fire, and the club he had wielded like a weapon, Ross had his doubts about that.

When they reached the pasture, they climbed through the gate rather than open it and give the goats an opportunity to escape. Curious, or maybe hoping for food, the goats gathered around them like children around a picnic table. Summer pushed through the animals and on to the broken fence.

They pulled out a tilting post and Ross dug the hole a foot or so deeper. Once the post was replaced in the hole, he shoveled the dirt back while Summer tramped it down with his foot. As they went on to the next fencepost, Summer began to ask questions.

"This man you saw in the barn—what did he look like?"

"I just got a glimpse of him. He wasn't too tall—about your height, maybe." Ross frowned, trying to recall the fleeting image he'd seen in the smoky firelight. "He wore a black hat low over his eyes. And he had on a blue and gray plaid shirt." He hadn't remembered the shirt until just now. "Do you know anybody who looks like that?"

"Only a couple dozen," Summer replied.

"Oh, and I found a matchbox, too," Ross said. "The man had been trying to light some more hay. The box says Blue Moon Café on the top."

Summer reached in his shirt pocket and pulled out a box identical to the one Ross had stowed away in his knapsack. "I reckon three-quarters of the men in this valley are carrying a box of matches from the Blue Moon." He dropped the box back in his pocket and wiped his shirt sleeve across his sweaty face. "The Blue Moon Café is on State Street in Greenwood Park. They serve the best peach pie this side of California."

Just then, Ross felt something tugging at his clothes and looked around. A goat with short, blunt horns and a wispy beard was chewing on the back of his shirt. When Ross wrenched away, a piece of material tore free. The unruffled animal chomped on his prize and stared at Ross without blinking.

"That fellow would eat the fender off of a car if you put a little salt on it," Summer said.

Ross went back to work but kept an eye on the inquisitive goats. He didn't have many clothes—only two shirts, since he couldn't wear the blue striped one anymore. Maybe Mary would offer to patch this one.

As he worked, Ross thought of the rumor about Summer burning down his house. Observing the quiet little man, Ross could not believe it was true. Still, his mother always said you couldn't judge the sweetness of a plum by the color of its skin.

"I wonder what makes a man set fires," Ross said.

"I reckon a person could have a reason," Summer replied. "When they catch this fellow, they can ask him. 'Course, they may never catch him."

"I wish now I'd followed him. I might at least have gotten a good look at him."

"It's better you didn't, Ross. The man might be dangerous."

"I'm not afraid of him," Ross murmured. He was just plain angry with the barn burner. Because of him, he had to hide like an outlaw.

After the last post had been set, they returned to where they had begun and Summer started unrolling the wire. He stopped and looked at Ross. "I left the staples back at the house."

"I'll go get them," Ross said. "Just tell me where to find them."

"They're in a brown paper sack. I think I left it on the kitchen table."

Ross returned to the house and slipped through the screen door into the small, dark kitchen. There was nothing on the round table except a sugar bowl. Once his eyes adjusted to the dimness, he spied the brown sack on the lower shelf of the cupboard. He crossed the room and was about to pick it up when something moved next to it. He jerked his hand away. The sudden motion sent him staggering backward and he fell against the table. His right foot struck a chair and it went spinning across the room. It took several seconds for Ross to regain his footing and for his heart to start beating again.

He approached the cupboard with more caution this time. The thing was in plain sight now, a huge brown spider, the biggest Ross had ever seen. It sat beside the staple sack as though it were guarding it.

Ross studied it for several moments, considering what to do. They couldn't fix the fence without

"When it gets tired of being moved around, maybe it will look for a new address."

Emily looked at him for a moment. Then warmth ignited in her eyes and spread outward to light her whole face.

Ross had never seen her smile that way at anyone except Hannah. He smiled back, wishing he could stay there and talk a little longer. But Jimmy was waiting for him. Just as he turned away, Emily spoke his name. He swung around to face her.

"Thanks," she said. Then, her face reddening, she hurried up the steps and into the house.

"You're welcome," Ross murmured to himself as he picked up the hammer and headed for the chickenhouse.

When he got there, Jimmy was pulling a rusty nail out of a piece of loose siding. In these hard times, people didn't spend money on new nails as long as they had used ones. A bent nail held better anyway, Ross remembered his father saying.

After the board was securely fastened over the hole in the roof, they went all the way around the building, nailing down loose boards. There was always the possibility a fox might come calling, Jimmy said. With the last piece of siding in place, they stood back to admire their work.

the staples. He had to get them somehow. He clapped his hands, hoping the noise would chase the spider away. But it remained as still as a rock.

Leaning closer, Ross glimpsed a tiny silver thread running from the paper sack to the cupboard door. Evidently he had interrupted the spider's web-building. Well, it would just have to spin its web somewhere else. He needed those staples.

Keeping the sack between him and the spider, Ross reached out and gently jiggled the silver thread. The spider ran at once toward the disturbance, and in that instant Ross grabbed the sack. His move broke the thread and sent the spider skittering back into a dark corner.

As Ross headed for the door, he remembered Hannah saying that Summer kept a pet lizard in his cupboard. The thing might have climbed into the staple sack. Ross pulled open the top and peered inside. There was nothing there but staples. He let out a loud breath and hurried toward the pasture.

Summer was squatting by the unrolled wire, bending and working the twisted pieces flat. "I forgot to warn you about Oscar," he said with a grin. "I hope he didn't scare you."

"All I saw was a spider."

"Oh, that's Amelia. Her job is catching the flies that get inside."

Ross smiled to himself, thinking of Hannah. Wait until she heard that Summer also had a pet spider.

Fastening the wire to the posts required teamwork. While Ross held the wire against the fencepost, Summer stapled it in place. Then they pulled and stretched the wire taut and nailed it to the next post. The goats sniffed and nosed the new fence, as if testing its strength. Summer pushed one away. "You mind your own business, or I'll have you for dinner one day."

By the time the repairs were completed, the sun was low in the west. Back at the house, Summer went into the kitchen and soon returned with a small basket of eggs, some speckled tan, some pale green.

He handed the basket to Ross. "If you're thinking I'll be telling people you were in the barn that night, you can be at peace. I don't intend to tell anyone about it." He grinned that tooth-missing grin. "And that includes my brother."

It was strange, but somehow Ross knew he could trust the man. "I'm much obliged," he said and hoped Summer understood how grateful he was for that trust. "And I thank you for the eggs," he added.

"You worked for them," Summer said. "You'll

be going by here every day or so. Stop in and visit. I talk to the animals, but they never tell me anything new."

Striding down the valley toward Mary's house, Ross heard singing from along the little stream. He recognized Hannah's voice. When he located her, she was knee-deep in water and elbow-deep in mud. She looked up and smiled. "Hi. I'm making mud bread."

The little cakes lining the bank did look something like Mary's bread loaves. Ross sat down to watch.

"Jimmy says this is brick clay," Hannah said. "Maybe I should make some bricks."

The bluish-gray mud resembled the dark clay they used at the brick plant to make the bricks. Ross picked up a handful and rolled it between his palms until he had a long, thin snake. It was fine and smooth and workable. Squeezing it into a ball again, he made a humped oval shape that reminded him of a turtle shell. If Hannah could make bread, he could make a turtle.

She came to watch while he added four short legs to the bottom, then a head and a pointed tail on opposite ends.

"Oh, a turtle! Can I have it, Ross Cooper?"

"Sure, in a minute." Ross picked up a stick

and made a shallow grid design on top. Then he handed the clay turtle to her.

"Thanks," Hannah said, holding it carefully in her palm. "When it dries, it'll be as hard as a rock. And I can keep it forever."

"Maybe not forever," Ross said. "It might crack when it dries."

"Hannah!" came Mary's distant call.

"Coming!" Hannah shouted back, then went back to the stream to rinse away the mud.

As the two of them walked along together toward the house, Ross told Hannah about the spider he had seen in Summer's kitchen. "Her name's Amelia."

"Do you think Summer Smith is crazy?" Hannah asked.

"No, I don't. He's just different."

"He gave me a pretty blue stone last year. I still have it. One time he gave Emily a sick baby bunny he found in the pasture. She cried when it died."

Ross tried to picture Emily crying, but all he could see was her defiant, flashing eyes as she argued with him or Jimmy.

As soon as they entered the kitchen, Hannah ran to show her mother the clay turtle. "Ross Cooper made it."

"It's nice, Hannah. You can put it there on the

windowsill to dry. Then I want you to wash up and change your clothes. Aunt Minnie has invited us to supper."

While Ross was washing, Mary came over to him. "Ross, I told Minnie about you being in Warner Smith's barn. She understands, and she wants me to be sure and tell you that you are welcome tonight."

"Thanks," Ross murmured, then decided to tell Mary that Summer knew, too.

"Summer is kindhearted," Mary said after he finished. "When I was first married—it was in the fall—he brought me two bushels of apples and a gallon of vinegar. His wife and daughter were still living then."

"I didn't know he had a wife and daughter. What happened to them?"

"It was the saddest thing. Summer got sick with influenza, and just as he started to get better, his little girl got it. Then his wife came down with it." Mary shook her head as if it was hard to speak of it. "They died in the same bed on the same day."

Ross thought of the little man he had worked with earlier, a man who had believed his story about the burning barn, a gentle, easygoing man who seemed happy. Then Ross remembered what Emily had said about him burning down his house.

"Did Summer really burn down a house?" he asked Mary.

"I couldn't say, because I wasn't there. All I know is that the day after he buried his wife and daughter his house burned to the ground."

"It could have been an accident," Ross said. "A crack in the chimney or something."

"Maybe. But people said Summer blamed himself for their deaths. They were everything to him."

"Mama, I can't do this," Hannah called. Mary went to help her button up her dress.

As Ross dried his hands and face, he thought about Summer and what he had lost. When you lose someone, someone you will never see again, it hurts. Ross had lost his family—not in the same way Summer had, but still they were gone. And for all Ross knew, they could have forgotten all about him by now.

NINE

When they were about to set off for Aunt Minnie's house, Jimmy and his mother discussed whether or not to take the lantern.

"It'll be dark when we come home," Jimmy said.

"But it's clear, and there's going to be a full moon tonight," Mary said. "We won't need it."

Ross knew Mary was trying to conserve kerosene because she wouldn't have money to buy any more. Whatever money she got would have to be spent on food. They left the lantern at home.

Jimmy skipped stones down the dusty road while Hannah picked a bouquet of dandelions. Ross couldn't help but overhear what Emily and her mother were saying to each other.

"You still haven't sewn the buttons on those two blouses, Emily."

"I hate sewing, Mama. Besides, when Jimmy loses a button, you sew it on for him."

"Girls should know how to sew on buttons, Emily."

"Why don't boys have to know?"

Mary turned and gave Emily a long look but did not answer.

"It's not fair, Mama, and you know it," Emily persisted.

Their conversation reminded Ross of the time when, before Sunday dinner, he had remarked that they should have gravy for the mashed potatoes. His mother responded by saying, "Come here. I'll show you how to make it."

"Boys don't cook," he had complained.

His mother had stared at him for a moment, then said, "Have they passed a law against that, too?"

He had learned how to make gravy, but he had never yet tried sewing on a button. It might be a good thing to know.

Aunt Minnie's house was small and, like the other houses they passed on the way, needed a coat of paint. But it seemed to float in a sea of color. Flowers bloomed around it, showing all the hues of the rainbow. Fragrance from the lilacs by the front steps wafted out to greet them.

Hannah and Jimmy were already seated in the porch swing when Aunt Minnie came through the door, wiping her hands on her apron.

"Supper's ready," she said and held the door open for them. She smiled at Emily, kissed the top of Hannah's head, and tousled Jimmy's sun-bleached hair. A warm hand lay for a moment on Ross's neck as he passed her. He was glad no one could see him swallowing the lump in his throat.

The meal was delicious, with new lettuce from the garden and fresh catfish a neighbor had brought that very morning. Strawberries in thick cream topped off the meal. While Ross was spooning up the last of the cream in his bowl, he thought back to the lunch Johnny Peale had brought to work. Could it have been lard that was spread on his bread to make a sandwich?

By the time supper was over, the sun had set. Aunt Minnie shooed Jimmy and Ross and the girls outside, reminding them not to run into the clothesline in the dark.

Lightning bugs sparked up from the grass just as a big yellow moon came climbing over the rim of the hill. Jimmy ran to the sycamore that spread leafy arms over the whole back yard. Clutching a limb, he swung up into the tree.

"Come on up, Ross."

Emily got there before Ross and reached for the limb Jimmy had used.

"No girls allowed," Jimmy called down.

"Just try and stop me," Emily said.

"Don't let her come up, Ross. Grab her!"

Ross was so stunned by the order that he simply stood there staring up at them. But Emily had stopped on her own. Her troubled eyes rested on him for a long moment; then she let go of the limb and dropped to the ground. Without saying a word, she walked away.

Ross never would have "grabbed" her, as Jimmy wanted, but Emily must have thought he might. She wandered off, head bowed, hands clasped behind her back, and just for a second Ross felt sorry for her. Then he remembered how she felt about him. She was too dangerous to pity.

"You coming up?" Jimmy asked.

Ross shook his head and walked back toward the house. He had climbed enough trees for one day. Settling on the porch steps, he watched Hannah capture lightning bugs, then, with a gentle lift of her hand, launch them back into the air. Emily was nowhere in sight.

When they got ready to leave for home, Mary had to call three times before Emily appeared. Aunt Minnie stopped them on the steps.

"I almost forgot, Mary. Mr. Morris has some sweet potato plants for you. He said he'd leave them on his back porch. As you can see, he's already in bed." She pointed at the house across the road, a shadowy hulk in the moonlight.

"Good. The boys can run over and get them right now." She turned to Jimmy and Ross. "The girls and I will go on ahead. After you get the plants, come straight home. Be quiet over there and don't wake Mr. Morris."

The lustrous moon lit the boys' way across the road and up the short lane. As they followed the well-worn path around the house, leafy trees shut out the moonlight, casting dusky shadows over them.

Jimmy was leading the way. "Be careful of that bucket," he whispered over his shoulder, but too late. Ross stumbled into the bucket and sent it clattering against the wall of the house. Smothering their laughter, the boys proceeded with more caution.

The burlap sack of plants lay in a patch of moonlight at the top of the porch steps. Jimmy went to get it while Ross waited, peering around him with rising uneasiness. The darkness seemed alive with strange sounds and vague, moving shapes. He told himself there was nothing there except shimmering moonlight and ragged tree shadows. But he shivered anyway.

Out of the corner of his eye, he thought he saw a glimmer of light, but when he turned to get a better look, it vanished. He could just make out the black bulk of an outbuilding under the trees. He jumped when Jimmy spoke.

"You ready to go?"

"Wait a minute. I thought I saw a light."

"It's probably the moon reflecting off of something," Jimmy said. "Come on. Let's get going."

Ross didn't move. "What if it's the barn burner trying to set another fire?"

"If it is, I don't want to be anywhere near. For one thing, Mr. Morris has—"

"But I'm pretty sure I saw a light. If there is someone, we should find out what he's doing." Despite the flutter in his stomach, Ross was more eager than afraid. This would be his chance to catch the barn burner! "Come on!" He started in the direction of the dark building, pulling Jimmy along with him.

"Ross, let's get out of here. I told, you Mr. Morris has—"

There it was again, a pinpoint of light near the building. Ross shrank back, bumping into Jimmy. The sudden rush of air from his lungs left him weak. Like a fish tossed up on dry land, his mind flopped this way and that, giving off silent warnings. *Watch out! Quick! Run!* But his legs were useless logs.

Suddenly, the silence exploded. Wood screeched against wood as an upstairs window flew open. A man shouted down at them. "What's going on? Who are you?" A dog's frantic barking added to the uproar.

Jimmy forced Ross to move, dragging him into the deep shadows alongside the house. "Come on! He's got a—"

Sudden thunder split the night.

"—a shotgun," Jimmy finished, then broke into a run.

Another deafening boom sent them tearing through the night like scared rabbits. Once in the road, they ran at breakneck speed and did not begin to slow until, staggering and panting for air, they finally collapsed. In the distance, they heard two more blasts.

Jimmy started laughing when he could get his breath. "I tried to tell you he had a shotgun."

Ross wiped the cold sweat from his forehead. "Do you think he'll come looking for us?"

"No. He doesn't leave the house after dark. He just shoots off his shotgun whenever he hears a noise. Doesn't even bother to aim." Jimmy giggled. "I bet he forgot all about leaving the plants for us."

"I wonder if it was the barn burner by the shed," Ross said.

"I don't think so. He would have run, too, when Mr. Morris started shooting."

"I guess you're right," Ross said. "I probably just imagined I saw a light. But I almost wish he had been there."

"What would you have done?" Jimmy asked. "Walked up and asked him his name?"

They both giggled this time. In the pale light, Ross could see Jimmy hugging the sack of sweet potato plants to his chest.

"We'd better get going," he said. "Your mother will be worrying."

They walked down the moon-silvered road, each lost in his own thoughts. Finally, Ross spoke. "I don't think we should tell your mother what happened."

"No," Jimmy agreed. "She'd just worry. She might decide that the only way to keep us safe is to tie us to a porch post."

Ross smiled, thinking how lucky he was to have found Mary's family. Jimmy had been his friend right from the start.

As they neared the house, they saw Mary and Emily on the porch. Mary jumped to her feet. "Jimmy, I was so worried. We heard something that sounded like a shotgun. Did you hear it?"

In the muted light, Ross and Jimmy exchanged glances. "We heard it," Jimmy said. "We figured it was thunder."

Mary made no comment about the cloudless, moon-bright night. "I thought maybe Mr. Morris woke up and thought you were intruders. He has that awful shotgun, and you were so late in coming. Well, you're safe. And it's bedtime," she added, crossing to the door. She went on into the kitchen, and soon light from the oil lamp lit the dark porch. Setting the sack of plants by the steps, Jimmy followed his mother inside.

Ross paused when he saw Emily, arms wrapped around a porch post, staring at him.

"It was Mr. Morris's shotgun we heard, wasn't it?" she said in a low voice.

Ross took a deep breath. "Yes, but we didn't want your mother to worry."

"You were right not to tell her. But if she doesn't let you out of her sight from now on, you can figure she probably knows."

Ross chuckled. "Yeah. Jimmy said she might tie us to a porch post."

Emily's quiet laugh surprised Ross, and before he knew it, he was telling her what had happened in Mr. Morris's back yard.

"Then there really is a barn burner." There was a softness in Emily's voice that Ross had never heard before.

"Yes, there is," he said. "And one of these days or nights, we'll run into him. We may even be lucky enough to catch him setting a fire."

"You'd better be careful," Emily said, moving over to the door. "Instead of you catching him, he might catch you."

Remembering Summer's warning about the barn burner, a sudden awful idea flashed into Ross's mind. What if Summer was the barn burner? He was about the same size as the man Ross had seen.

But that just couldn't be. A man wouldn't burn down his brother's barn, would he? Yet people in the valley accused Summer of burning down his own home. If he could do that, he would have no qualms about burning other people's buildings.

Though he hated the idea, Ross kept turning it over and over in his mind. He stayed on the porch after Emily went inside. And he was still there thinking about Summer when Mary came to remind him that he had to go to work at the brick plant the next day.

TEN

The next morning in the lamplit kitchen, Ross ate while Mary talked about the weather, her garden, and chickens.

"I'd like to have some chickens. A setting hen would get us going. But we don't even have a chickenhouse."

"How much does a setting hen cost?" Ross asked.

"I don't really know. The problem is, people don't want to part with their setters. If I had one, I certainly wouldn't give it up."

Ross thought of Mary's birthday. She'd have a chickenhouse soon enough, but the chickens might be hard to find. She was right. Why would people want to let go of something that provided them with eggs and a new brood of chicks every so often?

When he arrived at the brick plant, he spied Calvin beside one of the beehives. The kiln was empty, and a wagonload of unbaked bricks stood by the doorway. Calvin's first words were a curt command. "Grab a shovel and get those ashes cleared out. They want this kiln fired up by noon."

Ross watched Calvin walk on to the next beehive, where two men were removing the fired bricks and stacking them on a wagon. Men were busy everywhere around the plant, and Ross heard frequent laughter. Although Calvin was his usual, grumpy self, the rest of the men seemed happy to be working.

When the noon whistle sounded, Ross grabbed his lunch and headed for the shade. He took a seat beside Johnny Peale. "Thanks for telling me about the shortcut," he said.

"I reckon you met Summer Smith."

"Yes. I helped him fix his fence yesterday. The goats had trampled it down."

"He keeps the goats just for fun. He makes his living from his apples."

As Ross ate, he became aware of the conversation around him. The men were discussing a person called Jake. When someone mentioned a shotgun, Ross realized they must be talking about Mr. Morris.

"I guess when Jake's shotgun went off, people scattered."

"Did he hit anyone?"

"No, but the buckshot trimmed quite a few branches out of his big maple."

The men laughed.

News traveled almost as fast as Mr. Morris's buckshot, Ross thought. It had been only a few hours since he and Jimmy had streaked out of Mr. Morris's back yard, running for their lives.

"I wonder if they were the same fellows who've been burning barns around the valley."

"There isn't but one barn burner, and Warner Smith swears it's a boy."

Ross sneaked a glance at the man who had spoken. He was seated with his back against the tree, his legs stretched out in front of him. His green eyes, almost hidden beneath bushy eyebrows, reminded Ross of a watchful cat. The man finished rolling a cigarette, then clamped it between his teeth and reached for a match. When Ross saw the blue matchbox, his gaze flew back to the man's face. Could *he* be the one?

"The fellow might leave the valley, now that people are shooting at him," another man commented.

"Did you ever think that he might live here?" the man by the tree asked.

The quiet question made Ross even more suspicious. He squinted at the man. Was he the barn burner, and was he laughing to himself about fooling everyone?

"Yeah, it could be young Fred Marks. He's out every night looking for trouble," one of the men remarked.

"Tom Weaver's boy set their granary on fire last month, but Tom swears it was an accident," another man said.

Suddenly, it came to Ross that the barn burner might never be caught. People would go on believing a boy was setting the fires while the real barn burner could go undetected.

As the conversation turned to other things, Ross looked over and saw Johnny examining a grayish blue object about the size of his fist.

"What's that?" Ross asked.

Without speaking, Johnny handed it to him. Ross had never seen anything like it before. Fashioned from the same kind of clay used to make bricks, it was a lifelike replica of a frog. It had round, staring eyes, folded hind legs, and a tight-lipped mouth. Small raised spots dotted its back.

Ross rubbed a thumb over a bulging eye. The

piece was heavy, and sharp points of burned clay bit into his hand. Sitting in his palm, it looked almost real enough to hop away.

"You made this?" Ross asked.

"Yep. I make frogs, cats, dogs, and such. They aren't hard to do."

"Then they're baked, like the bricks," Ross concluded on his own.

"That's right. I just set them in one of the kilns that's about to be fired up. When the bricks are done baking, the animals are, too. You could make one."

"I couldn't make anything like this," Ross said, thinking of the crude turtle he had made for Hannah.

"All it takes is practice," Johnny said. "You just keep making them until you get a good one."

"Well, I might give it a try," Ross said.

The rest of the day Ross was so busy that he didn't have time to think about clay turtles or barn burners. But as he started home, he began to worry about meeting Summer. He didn't really believe Summer was the barn burner, but the idea just wouldn't go away. Would the man be able to tell what he was thinking? As he got closer, he began to hope Summer wasn't home.

Coming around the bend, he saw Summer sitting

on his front porch. Lady lay by his chair while the pups tumbled all around and over her. There was no way to avoid the meeting, so Ross walked right up to the porch.

"You hear about Jake Morris's shooting spree last night?" Summer asked, flashing his tooth-missing grin.

Ross nodded, not meeting the man's gaze for long. He hated his traitorous thoughts. He told himself Summer would never go around the countryside burning barns. Yet what if it were true that he had burned down his own house after his wife and daughter died?

Summer's voice pulled him back to the present. "I need to clean out my fruit cellar before the apples start coming. I thought maybe we could make another trade."

Ross hesitated only a second before accepting the man's offer. "I reckon I can help you. But I can't tomorrow. I have to help Mary."

"The day after will be fine," Summer said.

Suddenly, Ross remembered Mary talking that morning about getting a setting hen. Maybe he could make a deal with Summer, trade work for a setter.

"Mary's birthday is next week," he began, "and we're fixing up a chickenhouse for her. But she doesn't have any chickens. Yet." He paused, and inhaled a big breath. "I wonder if you would consider giving me a hen in trade, instead of eggs."

Summer slowly shook his head. "I only have two setters," he said. "I've had them for three years, and I just couldn't part with them." As Ross expelled the breath he had been holding, Summer continued. "But one of them is setting on some eggs right now. I could let you have the brood of chicks when they hatch. Then Mary could raise her own setters."

Ross was so tickled he couldn't do anything but grin.

"I'm not sure when they'll hatch," Summer said. "My setters always like to surprise me."

"It doesn't matter," Ross said. "As long as Mary gets some, she'll be happy. Thanks a lot. I'll be glad to work for them, whatever you think is fair."

A while later Ross set off for home, his spirits high, his steps light. Every so often he laid his hand against his pants pocket, as he had done a dozen times since leaving the brick plant. It was still there, his pay, three whole dollars, more money than he had ever had before in his life. Mary wouldn't want to take the money, but he would insist.

The moment the Barkley place came into view, Ross saw a vehicle parked beside the house. When he got close enough to see it clearly, it was too late to run. The people on the porch had already spotted him. They turned to watch his approach, Mary, Jimmy, Hannah, Emily, and the man in uniform.

As he drew nearer, Mary called out to him. "I'm glad you came, Ross, before Deputy Tillman left. He wants to talk to you."

Ross let out a slow breath when he saw that the lawman was not the one he had met on the road. He tried to smile a greeting, wondering if the rest of them could hear his heart pounding.

"Ross, I've already heard Jimmy's account of what happened last night," the man said. "Now I'd like to hear yours."

Ross shot a lightning glance at Jimmy, but when the boy merely shrugged his shoulders, Ross looked back at the deputy.

"Well, Mary told us to go over and get some sweet potato plants from Mr. Morris's back porch . . ." Ross related events exactly as they had occurred. Except he left out the part about a possible barn burner. He hoped Jimmy had not told that part either. When he had finished his story, the deputy nodded and turned to Mary.

"The boys were lucky. Jake Morris has been warned about shooting that shotgun when he doesn't know what he's shooting at."

"Yes, they were lucky," Mary said. But the gaze she turned on Jimmy told everyone there that the boy was not going to be lucky enough to avoid a scolding.

"You boys stay away from Mr. Morris," the lawman said as he turned to leave.

Even before the police car was out of sight, Mary was eyeing Jimmy. "You lied to me last night," she said.

"We didn't want you to worry, Mama. Besides, Mr. Morris missed us by a mile." Fidgeting under Mary's silent stare, Jimmy hurried on. "Ross wanted to see—"

Ross swallowed hard and spoke up. "I thought I saw a light."

Mary shook her head at them. "I guess it's partly my fault. I shouldn't have sent you over there after dark." Her arm slid around Jimmy's shoulders, and she pulled him close to her. With her cheek against Jimmy's hair, she looked across at Ross. "Promise me you'll be more careful when you're away from home."

Ross nodded, feeling a lump rise in his throat. His mother had hugged him sometimes the way

Mary was hugging Jimmy, tightly, almost desperately. Looking at the two of them, it seemed to Ross that he could feel his mother's arms around him. Just then, a small warm hand nestled into his.

"I dropped my turtle, Ross Cooper, and it broke all to pieces. Could you make me another one?"

Ross smiled down at Hannah. "Sure. When I get time." He wouldn't tell her that he might make one and bake it in a kiln. He would wait and see how it turned out.

"You're nice, Ross Cooper," she said, looking up at him. Her expression was innocent and earnest, and Ross squeezed her hand before letting go.

A tiny voice in the back of his mind told him that leaving Laurel Valley was not going to be as easy as he thought. If he were smart, he would just disappear one day and skip the sad goodbyes. But there were things he had to do here first. Even if he could forget about the barn burner, Mary needed his help a little longer. Besides, there was her birthday coming up.

After supper, when the dishes had been washed and the water bucket and woodbox filled, Mary called everyone to the back porch. She picked up the bag of sweet potato plants. "I'd like some help planting these," she said. "We'll need one to build mounds, one to carry water, one to set the plants."

"I'll carry water," Jimmy volunteered, grabbing a bucket and taking off for the stream.

Mary showed Ross how to pile the earth into high mounds with the hoe so that the plants would have the deep, loose soil they needed to thrive. He worked his way down the row, and Hannah followed, laying a fine-rooted plant on each mound. Emily came then, digging a hole with one hand and gently settling the plant into the pungent earth. Mary completed the setting process with a generous baptism of water.

Watching Emily work, Ross could tell she'd had plenty of practice setting out plants. She handled them as if they were fine pieces of china.

She looked up and saw him watching. Her face turned red and defiance flashed in her eyes. "Every girl needs to know how to set sweet potato plants. It's women's work."

"You mean, I'm doing women's work?" Ross said in mock horror. He caught a glimpse of a smile before Emily stepped over the mound, turning her back on him.

Grinning, Ross went back to work. Emily had spirit. She fought anyone who attempted to put any restraints on her. With her mother, she was honest and argumentative. With Jimmy, she never ceased to compete. She had been bluntly honest with Ross about the barn burnings. Only with Hannah was she gentle and affectionate. But maybe, just maybe, she was softening a little toward him.

Picturing Emily smiling at him, joking with him, maybe even teasing him made Ross's smile broaden. Just then, Hannah came over to him.

"What are you laughing about, Ross Cooper?"

Ross noticed Emily's back stiffen, and he knew she was waiting to hear his answer. "I was just thinking about a rainy day turning sunny" was all he said.

Just before heading to bed, Ross pulled out his money and offered it to Mary. She refused it.

"You'll need money to get back home," she said.

"I'm not going—" He had almost blurted out that he wasn't going home. "I'm not going to need any for a while," he said instead. "Besides, I'll be earning some every week."

When he kept insisting, Mary finally agreed to accept one dollar. "This will be enough for flour and salt and sugar. You save the rest for when you leave here."

It would help to have money when he went back on the road. But for a moment he thought how nice it would be to stay on, be a part of Mary's family. She hadn't asked him to stay indefinitely, though. Once the barn burner was caught, there would be no reason for him to remain.

ELEVEN

The next morning, following breakfast, Ross and Jimmy were given the chore of collecting firewood and stacking it by the back porch. Then they helped plant four rows of sweet corn and a row of peas. After that, they took turns with the sickle, cutting weeds all the way around the house.

When lunch was over, Mary came out and worked with the boys, trying to wrestle the front steps back into alignment. She used an ax handle as a lever while directing Jimmy and Ross how to lift and slide the stones into place. It was backbreaking work. When they were finished, Mary walked up the steps, then down again, smiling.

"Thank you very much," she said to them, as if they had done all the work. "You boys have earned a rest. Hannah and I are walking over to Aunt Minnie's, but we'll back before suppertime."

The boys had no intention of resting. As soon as Mary and Hannah were out of sight, they took the sickle and hurried across the stream to the brush-covered chickenhouse. Jimmy cut briars while Ross dragged them off and threw them on a pile for burning later. Ross told Jimmy about the deal he had made with Summer for a brood of chicks.

"But they may not be hatched by next week," he finished.

"That's all right," Jimmy said. "Mama will be so excited about the chickenhouse, she won't mind waiting for the chicks." After a moment's pause, he went on. "Summer is nice, and I wish people wouldn't call him crazy."

Ross recalled his own disloyal thoughts concerning Summer. "I got to wondering the other day if he might be the barn burner."

Jimmy snorted. "He isn't! He wouldn't do such a thing. And he didn't burn down his house, either."

Jimmy's angry defense of Summer made Ross feel better. He had never truly believed Summer was the barn burner.

With the brush cut away, the chickenhouse appeared to be solid, despite the loose siding and the hole in the roof. With a little work, it would soon be rainproof and safe from preying animals. They headed back to the house for hammer and nails and a piece of lumber to cover the hole.

Emily was on the back porch reading a book. She sat with her back against a post, one leg dangling over the edge of the porch floor. She didn't even glance up when they walked by. Ross had noticed that every time Emily went to Aunt Minnie's house, she came home with a book. It must be a good one, he thought, to keep her so absorbed.

While Jimmy crawled under the porch to look for boards, Ross went into the kitchen. He got a drink of water, then rummaged through a basket of tools until he found the hammer. There were a lot of old nails in the bottom of the basket, and he gathered up a handful and stuffed them in his pocket. Then he pushed through the screen door.

As he stepped out on the porch, what he saw snatched his breath away. He bent down and laid the hammer on the floor, then crept down the porch steps. As quietly as he could, he edged alongside the porch until he was only inches away from Emily.

Her head snapped up when she saw him so near, but Ross did not hesitate. He flung his arms around her, crushing the book between them, and in one swift motion swung her off the porch and out into the yard.

For a moment he was so flustered at what he had done that he forgot to let go of her. Finally, Emily began to squirm. And sputter. Then she found her voice.

"What in the world do you think you're doing? Let go of me!"

Ross's arms dropped away. He stepped back, feeling his face flush with heat. "I'm sorry. I saw a . . ." When words wouldn't come, he pointed to the porch.

Emily turned to look. Her mouth fell open and a gasp came from deep in her throat. There, where she had been sitting only moments ago, was a thick black snake. It was as big around as a water glass and at least three feet long. While they stared, it glided along the floor, curled around the post, then slithered down over the edge of the porch. Just as its tail disappeared, Jimmy came scooting out from under the other end of the porch, pulling a board behind him.

"I found one," he said. "It should be . . ." He stopped and looked from Ross to Emily. "What's wrong?"

"There's a snake," Emily said, pointing.

Jimmy scrambled to his feet. "Where? What kind of snake?"

"What does it matter what kind?" Emily said, wrinkling her nose. "A snake is a snake."

"It was a blacksnake," Ross said. "You must have stirred it up from the lumber pile. There it is."

"I'm going to get the hoe and kill it," Emily said.

"You are not!" Jimmy said. "A blacksnake won't hurt anybody. I'll take it over in the woods."

"It might crawl back and get into the house," Emily said and hurried for the hoe leaning against a tree.

Before she could return with her weapon, Jimmy had worked the board under the retreating snake and lifted it off the ground. Balancing it as if it were a fresh-laid egg, he headed for the stream. "Coming, Ross?" he called over his shoulder.

Ross started to follow but tripped over Emily's book. He picked it up and glanced at the title: *Elephants and Eagles.* Evidently she liked animals and birds. But she certainly didn't like snakes. He handed the book to her. "I'm sorry I scared you. It was too close to tell you to move."

Throwing her hoe aside, Emily reached for the book with trembling hands. "It ought to be killed. It'll come back, I just know it."

"If it does, we'll carry it off again," Ross said.

"Mama's going to love it," Jimmy said.

"What day is her birthday?"

"Next Tuesday. Four days from now. I sure wish Papa was going to be here. That would be the best birthday present Mama could ever get."

Yes, Ross thought, a family together was the way things should be.

They were lounging on the back porch when Mary and Hannah returned. Hannah ran up to them. "Look what Aunt Minnie sewed for us. A beanbag. Only it doesn't have real beans in it." The bag was made of bright blue and green material and small enough that Hannah could hold it in one hand.

"What's it for?" Jimmy asked.

"You play tag with it," Hannah told him, looking pleased that she knew something he didn't.

"Why doesn't it have beans in it?"

Mary spoke up. "If a person gets any beans these days, they're going to eat them, not play with them. Aunt Minnie used some of her beads in place of the beans."

Soft twilight drew them into the back yard after supper. Mary and Emily watched from the porch as Ross, Jimmy, and Hannah established two parallel lines, using trees as markers. Any person between those imaginary lines was eligible to be tagged.

Instead of chasing people, the one who was "it" threw the beanbag and tried to hit them. The person who was tagged then became it.

After throwing and retrieving the beanbag a dozen times or more without hitting the boys, Hannah stooped down to catch her breath. Emily came down the steps, hand outstretched. "Let me take a turn."

Hannah tossed her the bag and ran off, supposing she would be Emily's first target. But Emily spun around, looking straight at Ross. When she drew back her arm, Ross whirled to run. The bag hit him in the middle of the back.

As he bent to pick it up, he saw Emily turn away, smiling. From then on, the game had four players, until Mary came to make it five.

The next morning, the boys helped Mary dig up a row of half-buried stones that had at one time formed a walk from the front to the back porch. They were flat sandstones, laid down years before like stepping stones across a stream.

While they worked, Ross kept thinking of the first time he had seen the Barkley place. He had felt sorry for Mary that day, not really believing the house could be made livable. But in less than two weeks she had made it a home.

As he thought about it, he began to understand what he had never understood before. Home wasn't just a place. Home was an idea. It was an invisible circle that drew you in and made you feel you belonged. Mary had made this shabby place home, for her family and for Ross, too. But she could make any place into a home, he decided, because she carried the idea of home inside her.

These past days, shoveling ashes at the brick plant, lying in bed at night, Ross had felt a vague longing for the home he had left weeks before. Something pulled at him, making the idea of returning home sound almost reasonable. But he'd been banished. He couldn't go back. Could he? The nagging question was like an itch in the middle of his back that he couldn't reach.

After lunch, he set out for Summer's house, eager to get there and see if the chicks had hatched. There was no sign of Summer, but when Lady saw Ross coming, she started around the house, pausing at the corner as if waiting to escort him. Out back, Summer was just coming up the cellar steps and was carrying some bushel baskets.

"I figured you'd be along pretty soon," the man said. "I told Lady to watch for you."

"What do you want me to do?"

"The fruit cellar's at the bottom of the steps.

You can bring up all the baskets and crates. Then we'll sweep it out."

Ross lost count of the number of trips he made up and down the steps. Every container had to be rid of dried apples and leaves, and if a rotten apple had left a stain, it was scrubbed away with soapy water.

Finally, everything had been cleared out except for a long, wooden box resting on sawhorses in one corner. It was oak, Ross guessed, and smoothly finished; much too fine to be kept hidden away in this dark place. As he was speculating on what it might be, Summer appeared beside him.

"That's my coffin." When Ross's head snapped up, Summer laughed. "It makes a fine storage bin for my Rome Beauty apples."

So the tale about the coffin was true. Summer seemed to read Ross's thoughts. "I reckon that's one more reason why people call me crazy."

They dragged the coffin up the steps and into the sunshine. Then Summer scrubbed it inside and out until the yellow oak gleamed.

After the cellar's sandstone floor had been swept and the rafters cleared of cobwebs, they carried the clean baskets and crates back inside. And the coffin. Now Summer was all set for the season's first crop of fruit. They sat down on the back steps to rest.

Before Ross could ask about the chicks, Summer answered his question.

"That setter has been guarding her nest like it's a chest of gold. It shouldn't be long now."

"I'm mighty grateful that you're letting me work to pay for them. But today's work isn't enough. Do you have any other jobs that you want done?"

"There is something else, Ross. You see that dead tree out by the barn? I want to cut it up for firewood. If you can help, that and the work you did today will be plenty enough to pay for the chicks."

Too excited to sit still, Ross jumped up, grinning. "I'll be glad to help with the tree, whenever you say. Do you want to do it today?"

"No, Ross. I'm not as young as you. We'll save that for another day."

Ross went away, wondering how he could ever have thought Summer might be the barn burner. The little man helped his friends and neighbors and had a kindly way about him that a barn burner would never have. Besides, what reason could he have for burning barns?

Everyone was busy when Ross arrived at the house, because Aunt Minnie was coming for supper. He just had time to whisper to Jimmy that the chicks had not yet hatched before they both were put to work.

Ross was given the task of cleaning some strawberries Mr. Barkley had brought earlier. They looked and smelled delicious, and he was tempted to eat one. But he had learned that during hard times like these a person did not eat food that was meant for the family table. That would be stealing.

During the dessert of strawberries and ginger cookies, Aunt Minnie mentioned Mr. Morris. She laid an arm around Jimmy's shoulders and smiled down at him. "I'd never have allowed you boys to go over to his house the other night if I'd thought he would wake up and start shooting that gun of his."

"He wasn't shooting at us, Aunt Minnie," Jimmy said. "He was just making sure his gun was in working order. Besides, he couldn't hit a barn on a sunny day."

"Well, he might have hit you by accident," Aunt Minnie said. "With all these barn burnings, people are getting jumpy. I've been studying over who might be setting the fires. Whoever it is, he knows where all the old sheds and barns are located. It must be someone who lives here in the valley."

Ross remembered the man at the brick plant who had said almost the same thing. How could they ever identify the barn burner if he lived here, if people knew him as a neighbor? It gave Ross a spooky feeling, knowing he was the only one in the valley who had seen the man.

"You boys be careful when you're out and about after dark," Aunt Minnie said.

"They won't be out after dark anymore," Mary said.

"Aw, Mama! I was just going to ask if Ross and I could walk Aunt Minnie home," Jimmy said.

"No," Aunt Minnie spoke up. "I can walk home alone. It's not even a mile." She rose to her feet. "But I'd better be going. It's getting dark, and I didn't bring a lantern."

Lightning bugs flashed up out of the grass as Aunt Minnie passed by. She had just reached the road when she suddenly stopped and shouted back toward the house. "Mary, come quick!"

They all rushed out to where Aunt Minnie stood with an arm raised, pointing at the red glow in the evening sky.

"Something's burning, and it looks like it's awfully close to my house."

TWELVE

Aunt Minnie took off, striding fast. The others followed, nobody speaking, but all of them watching the red cloud grow brighter by the minute. Aunt Minnie set a frantic pace down the main road, and the others sometimes had to run to keep up. When she reached the point where she could see her house, she stopped. The roof was still there, the walls were intact, and there was no sign of flames.

"It's Bill Adams's barn," Jimmy said, pointing to the smoke cloud hovering over the pasture field next to Aunt Minnie's house.

"I've been worrying about that old barn," Aunt Minnie said, fanning herself with her big straw hat.

"I wonder if Mr. Adams's mare got out," Jimmy

said. "He usually fastens her in the shed next to the barn."

Aunt Minnie turned to Mary. "You've walked this far. You might as well come along and see what's happening."

People watching the fire from porches and yards nodded to Aunt Minnie and Mary as they passed. The barn, in plain view now, roared with a fury of well-fed flames. Two men had walked out into the pasture and were standing as close to it as they dared, silhouetted against the blazing structure.

Sparks shot high into the sky from the mountainous blaze, flaming back to earth like falling stars. Jimmy motioned for Ross to follow him and they climbed through the barbed wire fence.

"Don't get too close," Mary called after them.

Ross had not stayed to watch Warner Smith's barn burn. In fact, he had never seen such a fire before. It was awesome and scary at the same time. Heat reached out, dry and intense, burning his face and arms. He took a step backward and bumped into someone. "I'm sorry," he murmured. Turning, he saw it was Johnny Peale. Beside him was another man Ross had seen working at the brick plant.

Johnny smiled at Ross, then looked back at the barn. "Too late to save it now," he said. "When a fire gets that big, nobody can stop it."

"We thought it was Aunt Minnie's house at first," Jimmy said.

"The only things that seem to be burning in this valley are barns," Johnny said.

"You think someone set this fire?" Ross asked.

"I'd bet money on it," Johnny replied. "That fire had a real good start before anyone noticed it."

"Why do people burn barns?" Ross asked, not really expecting an answer.

"It won't hurt the farmers to suffer a little," Johnny said. "The rest of us barely have enough to feed our families, while the farmers' pantries are full."

Johnny's words, and especially his angry tone of voice, surprised Ross. The man didn't seem a bit concerned that Bill Adams was losing the only barn he had on his farm.

"There goes the roof," Jimmy said.

The collapse was almost like an explosion. A great, swelling cloud of ashes and sparks drove the two men by the barn backward until they stood beside Jimmy and Ross.

"Did you get your mare out, Mr. Adams?" Jimmy asked the man leaning on a pitchfork.

"Yes, I did, Jimmy. As soon as I opened the door, she took off running." Mr. Adam's pulled a hankerchief out of his pocket and wiped his eyes, then looked at the man next to him and shook his head.

"What am I going to do when bad weather comes? I can't afford to build a new barn."

Jimmy turned to Ross and whispered, "He raised her from a foal. She has a pretty blazed face and two white stockings. I rode her once last summer."

Mr. Adams pointed toward a clump of trees in the distance. "There's the mare. You want to go get her, Jimmy? She has her halter on."

"Sure," Jimmy said. He tapped Ross on the shoulder and the two of them walked toward the grove of trees.

Ears raised, eyes glittering, the mare was gazing at the fire so intently that she didn't even notice the boys at first. When they got close, Jimmy began talking to her in a crooning, sing-song voice. "Hey, there, girl. It's all right. The fire can't hurt you now. Easy, girl."

The mare backed away from his outstretched hand, snorting, stomping a front foot.

"Come on, girl. I won't hurt you," Jimmy said.

Terror gleamed in her white-rimmed eyes. She reared backward, slamming into a tree trunk, then veered away into the shadows.

"She's really scared," Jimmy said.

"Maybe we'd better let Mr. Adams catch her."

"No, she knows me," Jimmy said. "Once I get

ahold of her halter, she'll quiet down. Come on."

They followed, trying not to make any sudden movements that would drive the animal farther away. But every time they drew near, she tossed her head and pranced out of reach. The burning barn was no longer in sight, though clouds reflected the distant glow, making the shadowy woods seem even darker.

"Where did she go?" Ross asked in a hushed voice.

"Straight ahead," Jimmy said. "Listen."

They paused, holding their breath, trying to catch a sound of the animal's movement.

"There she is," Jimmy said, pointing. "You go around that way and make some noise. She'll come back toward me, and I can catch her."

"Be careful she doesn't run over you," Ross said.

Still unable to see the mare, Ross went off the way Jimmy had pointed. He peered into the shadows, but there was no sign of the animal and no sound to direct him. A gust of wind stirred the leaves over his head; then it grew so quiet he could hear the sound of something creeping through the grass. Feeling his way around a clump of prickly bushes, he stopped, his nerves tingling. He'd never known that the woods were so dark at night.

Suddenly, a black shape reared up right in

front of him. He let out a yelp and fell backward into the bushes, his heart fluttering, his legs churning. *Get up! Get away!* But he couldn't even get on his feet.

"Didn't mean to scare you," said a familiar voice.

Ross gasped for air, finally squeaking out the name. "Summer!"

"Is that you, Ross? It's so dark in here, it's like being a mile inside a coal mine without a lantern."

"You scared me!" Ross's legs were still trembling. Summer grabbed one of his arms and pulled him erect.

"What are you doing out here in the dark, Ross?"

"Jimmy and I were looking for Mr. Adams's mare. She ran away from the fire."

"I saw the light in the sky from my front porch," Summer said, "and figured it must be a big fire. Thought I'd come and take a look."

"It's Mr. Adams's barn. The fire is too big to put out so everyone's just watching it burn."

"I know. I watched a while, too."

Just then, Jimmy's call came out of the darkness. "Ross, I got her! Come on back."

"You go along," Summer said. "I'm going over the hill to home. See you in a day or so." In only seconds the little man had disappeared.

Ross turned in the direction of Jimmy's call and cupped his hands around his mouth. "Jimmy!"

"Over here" came the instant reply, closer than Ross had expected.

Working his way through the trees, Ross heard Jimmy's crooning voice even before he saw the mare. The horse had settled down, and stood quietly under Jimmy's gentle stroking. Ross approached slowly so as not to frighten her, then reached out and patted her sweaty shoulder.

"I thought maybe you were lost," Jimmy said.

"No, I was talking to Summer." Ross still felt shaky from Summer's sudden appearance.

"Summer! What's he doing out here in the woods?"

"He said he saw the light and wanted to see what was burning. Just like everybody else, I reckon."

"Hey, I bet Mama's looking for us," Jimmy said. "Come on."

The fire's light led them back to the pasture, where people still stood talking and eyeing the dwindling flames. Mr. Adams smiled wearily when the boys walked up with the mare.

"Good job, Jimmy. Is she hurt?"

"No, I don't think so," Jimmy said. "But she's still awful scared."

"You and your friend can come over one of these days and take a ride on her. After she's had a few days to forget about the fire."

"Thanks, Mr. Adams. We'd like that," Jimmy said, rubbing the mare's lathered neck.

Emily came walking up to them. "Jimmy, Mama said to come on. We're going home."

They crossed the pasture and slipped between the barbed wires to where Mary and Hannah were waiting.

"Where have you boys been?" Mary demanded.

"We went to catch Mr. Adams's mare," Jimmy said. "She ran away from the fire."

"Jimmy, you seem determined to make me worry. If your father were here . . ." She stopped, then turned abruptly and walked off, carrying the lantern Aunt Minnie had lent her. Emily and Hannah were close behind. Jimmy looked at Ross and shrugged his shoulders; then they ran to catch up to the moving circle of lantern light. The acrid smell of smoke followed them all the way home.

While Mary and the girls bathed, Jimmy and Ross sat on the back porch talking. "The mare sure was scared," Jimmy said.

"She wasn't the only one," Ross replied. "When Summer stood up in front of me in the woods, I thought I never would get my breath."

Jimmy laughed, but his next words were serious. "That's the third barn to burn in the last month."

"And the barn burner could have been standing there with everyone else, watching it burn," Ross said, "because nobody knows who he is."

"I don't think he'd have the nerve to be right there in the open," Jimmy said. "But he may have been hiding close by."

"Maybe it's somebody we know," Ross said. He looked at Jimmy and realized they were thinking the same thought. *Summer!* It was strange, the man being out there alone in the woods. But he could have come, as he had told Ross, just to check on the fire. Being near the burning barn didn't mean Summer had done the burning. How well Ross knew that!

"I don't think he did it," Jimmy said.

"Neither do I," Ross said, wanting to believe his friend was innocent.

When the boys had the kitchen to themselves, they emptied the washtub and refilled it, then raced to see who could undress and get into the tub first. Jimmy won. After he had finished, he gave Ross a quick salute and went off to bed.

The lamp's flickering light soothed Ross's mind as the warm water soothed his body. He was so lucky, he told himself, to have a home, even if it was only temporary. He stepped out of the tub, toweled himself dry, and slipped on his trousers. Flinging his shirt over one shoulder, he leaned over and blew out the lamp. He would have to wait until morning to empty the bathwater, when Jimmy could help.

Once his eyes had adjusted to the darkness, he started up the stairs. But he stopped suddenly, glimpsing movement above. He stepped back into the kitchen to let Emily go by.

"I'm thirsty," she murmured in passing, as if she had to give him a reason for being there. Ross thought of several teasing replies but kept silent instead.

Across the room, the tin dipper rattled against the water bucket. Then Emily spoke from the shadows. "I'd like to . . . to say I'm sorry for thinking you were the barn burner."

Ross drew in a slow breath. "Well, I *was* in Warner Smith's barn when it was burning," he said.

Emily ignored his remark. "And I think it's nice that you're giving Mama some chicks for her birthday."

"They may not be here for that day, but Summer says it won't be long."

"Setting hens are like horses and cows; calendars don't matter to them."

"They don't matter much to me either," Ross said, "except at Christmas."

Emily was a white ghost moving across the kitchen. Just as she slipped past him, she whispered, "Sweet dreams," then went running up the stairs.

Ross followed at a slower pace, grinning to himself in the darkness.

THIRTEEN

Sunday breakfast was leisurely and late. Mary made buckwheat pancakes, which disappeared as fast as she could fry them. Afterward, she sent Jimmy to the spring for water and Hannah and Emily to the attic to look for a basket she could use to bring back some canning jars from Aunt Minnie's.

When Mary began washing the dishes, Ross took a dish towel from the wooden rack behind the stove and began drying.

"Ross, I've been wanting to talk to you," Mary said without looking up. She washed two more plates while he waited.

He was sure she was going to tell him he had to leave. He should have expected it. She had invited him to stay because she needed help settling into the house. Then she had offered to hide him from the law. Maybe she was tired of worrying about him, tired of wondering when the sheriff would come to arrest him. She might even get in trouble with the law herself. After all, she was hiding a fugitive. Ross could understand why she would want him gone.

Drying her hands on her apron, Mary walked over and sat down at the table. She folded her hands on the tabletop and studied them for several seconds. At last she looked up at him. "You ought to go home, Ross."

He looked away. He had the sudden urge to tell her about his family, about the fight they'd had and his angry flight from home. Before he could stop them, the words came tumbling out. "I can't go home. They don't want me there."

Mary's eyes gleamed like midnight stars. "A person can always go home."

Dropping into a chair, Ross spread his hands flat on the table and leaned toward her. "You don't understand. They ordered me to leave."

Mary leaned forward, too. "Sometimes parents speak too quickly. They don't always mean what they say."

"My mother meant it," Ross murmured. The words still echoed in his brain: "Get out of my sight!"

He doubted if he would ever stop hearing them. He willed himself not to think about that night.

"I don't know what happened between you and your parents, Ross, but one thing I know for sure. They need you."

Ross laughed out loud at her remark. "They don't need me! They've got Tom and Amy and the others. They're big enough to do the work around there."

"Ross, it isn't that they need you just to work. They need you to be part of their life."

Ha! They needed him like they needed a hole in their roof. At least Mary had not said he needed them! He didn't need any of his family. He had proved this past month on the road that he could get along very well without them. He looked at Mary and shook his head. One thing he knew for sure. He wasn't going home again.

Mary breathed a quiet sigh. "Every time I look at you, Ross, I visualize your mother wondering where you are and how you are."

"But she's the one who told me to get out."

"She was just speaking in the anger of the moment," Mary said. When Ross did not answer, she reached out and grasped his hands. "She didn't mean for you to go forever. Don't let angry words keep you away. You can go home."

Even as he felt his certainty slipping away, Ross whispered, "I can't!"

Then a painful thought flashed into his mind. Was Mary trying, in a polite way, to tell him to leave? She was having a hard time feeding her family, and now that her husband couldn't send her any more money, it would get even harder. Suddenly, Ross knew deep inside that it was time to go. They'd be better off without him. Besides, he was getting too attached to this place.

"I've been thinking I should get back on the road," he said without looking at her.

"But if you don't go home, where will you go?"

"I'll find work somewhere."

"You've got work here," Mary said softly.

Something in her voice told him she hadn't been hinting for him to leave, after all. She just wanted him to go home because she cared about him. He hung his head and swallowed hard.

Footsteps thumped across the porch. Squeezing Ross's hands once more, Mary rose from the table and went back to washing dishes.

Jimmy came through the door and set the water bucket down. "You want to walk up to see Summer Smith's puppies?" Jimmy asked Ross. Then, making sure his mother was not looking, he mouthed the word "chickens."

"Sure," Ross replied. "Summer is always happy to have visitors."

"Don't you bring back any puppies," Mary told them. "We can't afford to feed them."

"I want to go see the puppies," Hannah said, coming into the kitchen ahead of Emily. "Can I, Mama?"

Jimmy snorted. "No, you can't."

"I think it would be all right for her to walk along with you boys," Mary said.

"I'll go, too," Emily spoke up.

Jimmy groaned. "Mama! We don't want girls tagging along."

Mary merely smiled at him, then turned to Emily. "You can take Summer a loaf of that bread I baked yesterday."

Walking up the valley, Emily took the lead, Hannah running to keep up with her. When they climbed through the fence into Sweet Spring Road, Emily said in a low voice that only Ross could hear, "Let me know if you see any barn burners." Then she ran off, leaving him staring at her retreating back. She was actually teasing him.

Summer came out of the house when he heard them at the front porch. The puppies were growing bolder. One even crept over to sniff Jimmy's outstretched fingers while Lady watched.

"We came to see if the eggs have hatched," Ross said to Summer.

"Mama sent you this bread," Emily said, handing over the paper-wrapped loaf.

"That's mighty kind of your mother. Tell her I'm obliged." Summer was smiling when he took the bread inside and still smiling when he returned to the porch. "Let's go see about those eggs."

He led them to the small barn, which appeared to depend on the wild cherry tree beside it to hold it up. Boards curled away from the walls like pale gray ribbons. Holes too numerous to count peppered the tin roof. Ross mused that even the barn burner would likely refuse to waste his fire-making talents on such a dying structure.

They stood back and watched as Summer walked over to the nest. The hen regarded him with shiny-eyed defiance. When he tried to reach under her, she pecked at his hand, but he was too quick for her. They played their sparring game, Summer reaching, the hen striking, Summer retreating, until finally he broke the rhythm and grabbed the setter. He lifted her off the nest, then after a moment gently set her back. She waggled from side to side several times before settling down over her precious hoard.

"Nope. None hatched yet," Summer said. "I'll

keep an eye on her. When is your mother's birth-day?"

"Day after tomorrow," Jimmy said.

"You stop by tomorrow after work, Ross. Maybe they'll be pecking their way free by then," Summer said.

As they walked back to the house, Lady came to meet them, the pups bounding alongside.

"Now," Summer said, looking at Ross, then at Jimmy and the girls, "can I give each of you a pup? Or will one be enough for all of you?" He scooped up one of the wriggling pups and handed it to Hannah.

"Mama says we can't have one because we can't feed it," Jimmy told him.

Summer sobered at once. "Times are hard right now. What do you hear from your papa?"

"He's still in Colorado," Jimmy said. "He broke his leg."

"He'll be coming home one of these days," Emily hurried to add.

"And when he does," Hannah piped up, "then we can get a puppy."

Ross listened to the way they talked of their father coming home, as if they were announcing Christmas. Sudden longing for his own home swelled inside of him until he thought he would burst. He turned away from the others, trying to remember the familiar anger. He couldn't go home again! But Mary's words came whispering through his mind. "A person can always go home."

After playing awhile with the puppies, Ross and the others set out for home. Along Sweet Spring Road, Jimmy pointed out an old barn in a grove of trees. "The barn burner hasn't found that one yet."

"Pretty soon there won't be any barns left around here," Hannah declared.

"Don't worry," Emily told her. "The man is going to make a mistake one of these days. Then he'll go to jail."

"Did you ever think that maybe it's a girl setting all these fires?" Jimmy said to her.

"Girls aren't that dumb," she told him, her eyes sparkling as they met Ross's.

"I like to watch the fire in Aunt Minnie's fireplace," Hannah said. "Sometimes the flames are red, and sometimes they're blue."

"See there!" Jimmy said. "She likes fire. Hannah, have you been burning down barns?"

Hannah ran to grab him, but he danced out of her reach. She kept after him, chasing him down the shady road, leaving Emily and Ross to walk along side by side. After several moments of comfortable silence, Ross spoke up. "I'm taking your advice." When Emily looked up with a question in her eyes, he continued. "I'm leaving next week."

Emily didn't say anything at first, but her expression turned solemn and thoughtful. "I thought you wanted to find out who's burning the barns."

Ross gazed down the road, thinking of Summer Smith. If Summer was the barn burner, Ross didn't want to catch him, did not even want to be in the valley when he was caught. "It may take a long time, and I need to be going."

"You'll be here for Mama's birthday, won't you?"

"Yes. I'll work two more days at the brick plant. And I promised to help Summer cut down a tree."

Emily bent to pick up a speckled stone out of the road. "You know, you don't have to leave now. Nobody thinks you're the barn burner anymore."

"I have to leave sometime," Ross said, thinking of how his life would change. Going back on the road meant being hungry, bathing in a stream, sleeping on the ground, walking from daylight till dark.

"Are you going home?" Emily asked.

"No." The answer was blunt and final. That one word, along with the look on Ross's face, silenced her. They did not say anything else the rest of the way home.

Afternoon grayed into a cloudy dusk, and the regular after-supper tag game ended when a blustery storm descended on them. They sat on the porch, enjoying the rain, before they went to bed.

Rising in the first light of dawn, Ross looked out the window at the still misting rain. It was going to be a wet, uncomfortable walk to work. He wore his hat, though it did little more than keep the rain out of his eyes. By the time he reached the brick plant, he was soaked to the skin.

Before reporting to Calvin, Ross went by the plant office. Seeing him in the doorway, Mr. Weston motioned him inside. "What can I do for you, Ross?"

Ross pulled off the dripping hat. "I came to tell you I'm leaving Laurel Valley next week. I'm much obliged for the work you gave me."

"Calvin's told me what a good worker you are. I'm sorry to lose you, Ross. If you're ever around looking for work, come and see me," Mr. Weston said. "And be sure to stop back for your pay."

Ross nodded and turned away. So Calvin was not such a mean character after all. He just wanted people to think he was.

Approaching the beehives, Ross realized he had forgotten all about making Hannah a turtle. Maybe he could get some raw clay and shape one during his lunch break. Johnny Peale might even help him. Then he could put the turtle in a kiln and pick it up when he came back for his last pay.

At noon, carrying a glob of moist clay in one hand and his lunch in the other, Ross went and sat down beside Johnny.

"I promised I'd make someone a turtle. Will you show me how?"

"Let's see what you can do first," Johnny said.

Laying his lunch aside, Ross kneaded the clay until it was smooth and pliable, then began shaping it. Johnny helped him with occasional suggestions.

"Don't make the legs quite so long. They'll collapse under the weight of the body."

A little later, he said, "The outer edge of the shell turns up a little."

When Ross set the finished piece in the grass, Johnny reached out and gently gave the turtle's head a little squeeze just below its eyes. Ross was amazed. The man knew exactly what to do to make it more lifelike. Now it was perfect.

"Good job, Ross. It's all ready to burn."

As he was going back to work, Ross saw some men carrying bricks into one of the beehives. He headed in that direction, holding the soft turtle as gently as if it were a live butterfly. He paused in the open doorway. A man in a dust-covered shirt looked up and saw him.

"What can I do for you, son?"

"I made this turtle, and I'd like to leave it here to be fired. Would that be all right?"

"Sure. Set it on the ledge there by the door." The man pulled a handkerchief from his rear pocket and wiped his forehead. "You been taking lessons from Johnny Peale?"

"He helped me," Ross said, leaning over and placing the turtle on the brick ledge. "But it's not as good as what he makes."

"Well, he's had lots of practice. With eight kids, there's always a birthday coming up."

"Does he sell any?" Ross asked, thinking if his turtle didn't turn out right, he might be able to buy an animal from Johnny.

"Not anymore. People won't buy knickknacks when they don't even have enough money for food."

"I'll be back to get this day after tomorrow," Ross told the man.

"It'll be here," the man said, grinning, "hard enough to last a hundred years."

Ross grinned back. "If I don't drop it."

FOURTEEN

At the supper table, there was a simmering energy Ross could feel. Hannah jabbered on and on, interrupting anyone else who tried to talk. Jimmy could not sit still, and Mary told him several times to quit squirming. Though Emily hardly spoke, her smile was as bright as the afternoon sun coming in the window. Mary might have guessed the reason for their barely concealed excitement, but she never let on.

The four of them played beanbag tag until dark, pausing one time to rest and review the plans for the next day.

"Are you sure Aunt Minnie has all the makings for a cake?" Jimmy asked Emily.

"Don't worry about the cake. When Aunt

and I come tomorrow, we'll have it. And
s, too."

annah, don't forget to give me your red hair
," Jimmy said. "We'll tie it on the chicken-
door first thing in the morning."

e got another present for Mama," Hannah
I made her a flower vase out of some clay
he stream."

ss smiled, remembering the day he had
Hannah up to her elbows in the mud.

hat about the chickens?" Emily asked.

stopped by, but they haven't hatched yet," he
er. "Summer said if they hatched tonight,
he'd bring them over tomorrow."

Ross recalled the chicken he had earned working for Mr. Myers. He had wanted it to be a surprise for the family, but it had turned out all
wrong. Well, this time things would be different.
When Mary learned where the chicks had come
from and what he'd done to pay for them, she
would believe him and accept them. He couldn't
wait to see her face!

Mary's birthday began unfolding early the next
morning. They sang "Happy Birthday" to her
first thing, then made her sit down while they
cooked breakfast. She was not allowed to do the

dishes but instead was given a package to unwrap, the clay vase Hannah had made for her. Jimmy told her that he and Ross were going to clean out the weeds from the garden. And Emily's gift was scrubbing both porches.

They set to work, and by lunchtime every weed was gone from the garden, leaving rows of tiny vegetables bright green against the chocolate-colored earth. The porches and steps were clean, and firewood and water had been carried in. Mary, relaxing with a basket of mending, exclaimed over every completed task.

In late afternoon, Emily and Aunt Minnie arrived. Besides the cake concealed in a covered basket, Aunt Minnie had brought lettuce from her garden and fresh-picked raspberries.

After they finished eating dinner, they made Mary close her eyes while they brought out the cake. Aunt Minnie had found only three tiny candles, but once they were lit, they brightened all the faces around the table. They sang "Happy Birthday" again, and then Mary blew out the candles and pulled them from the cake. When she handed them to Jimmy, he carefully licked the icing off each one before passing it to Aunt Minnie. She said she would save them for the next birthday.

Pieces of cake were cut and eagerly devoured. Then Jimmy, chosen as spokesman, told his mother about the brood of chicks she would be getting in the near future.

"We kept hoping they'd hatch before today, Mama," he said, "but I guess you can't hurry a setting hen."

"If we're going to have chickens," Mary said, looking surprised, "then we'll have to have a chickenhouse."

Jimmy jumped to his feet. "Come with us, Mama. We have something to show you." He pulled her toward the door, then led the way through the yard and across the stream. He stepped aside so that she could see Hannah's red ribbon decorating the door latch.

Mary's eyes sparkled, and she hurried forward to lift the latch. "It's wonderful," she said. "Just what I've wanted." She examined the weathered building inside and out, noticing everything, the repaired roof, the nailed siding, the box nests. She grabbed Jimmy and embraced him, then went and squeezed the girls against her. Still smiling, she stepped over and gave Ross a quick hug. "It's wonderful!"

Tears burned in Ross's nose and throat. Even if Mary was partial to boys, as Emily had said, she had not taken Ross into her home just for that reason. She had liked him from the beginning, he knew, just as he had liked her from that first day when she reminded him of an ironwood tree. And somehow she had made him feel that he belonged there. Leaving her would be a lot harder than leaving Laurel Valley.

As they were walking back to the house, Hannah pointed up the valley toward Sweet Spring Road. "Look! There's a man coming."

"It's Summer," Jimmy said. "Maybe he's bringing the chicks."

But they could see he wasn't carrying anything. His pace was steady and slow, and Ross wished he would hurry with his news, whatever it was. When Summer reached them and nodded without speaking, Jimmy blurted out the question everyone wanted answered. "What about the chicks?"

"That's why I'm here," Summer said, pulling off his stained straw hat and swiping the back of his hand across his forehead. "I have bad news. Last night, I heard a commotion in the barn. By the time I got there, a raccoon had cleaned out the nest."

They were all too stunned to speak. Jimmy kicked at a clump of grass, and Emily laid an arm around Hannah's sagging shoulders. But then Summer grinned, reached into a bulging shirt pocket, and pulled out three fluffy yellow chicks.

"These got knocked out of the nest, but I found them before the raccoon did."

Emily and Hannah surged forward, gathering the tiny birds into cupped hands.

"You have to feed and water them," Summer said, "until they can learn to scratch up some food on their own."

"We'll keep them in a box by the stove," Mary said. "It was nice of you to bring them over, Summer. Come in and have a piece of my birthday cake."

After Aunt Minnie and Summer left, a game of beanbag tag was launched, with Mary the most enthusiastic player, and the most accurate.

The next day, Ross left after breakfast to go help Summer cut down his dead tree. He found him on the back porch, sharpening a long jagged-toothed saw with stubby wooden handles on each end. As the whetstone rasped against the steel, Summer explained the task to Ross.

"The best way to fell a tree is to let the saw do the work. Pull, don't push. When I pull, you just go along for the ride."

The shiny saw blade sliced through the dead wood in only minutes. With a slow, creaking movement, the tree toppled and crashed to the ground. Using an ax and a short-handled saw, they cut up the wood, then stacked it by the back porch. When they were finished, Summer got them each a glass of cold water.

"So you're leaving, Ross. Heading home?"

"I'm leaving, but I'm not going home."

Something in his voice made Summer pause a moment before speaking. "Well, as long as you keep in touch with your family," the man said.

"A person doesn't really need a family," Ross said. "Look at you. You get along all right by yourself."

Leaning back against a porch post, Summer gazed out across the field where the goats grazed. At last he spoke. "A family is kind of like a picture puzzle, Ross. All the pieces fit together to make something special. When pieces are missing, the puzzle is never complete."

Ross didn't know what to say, so he waited for Summer to go on. When he continued, his voice was so soft that Ross had to strain to hear him.

"My wife and my three-year-old daughter died nine years ago. I get along all right, as you say, but the pieces are still missing."

A sadness settled over Ross, as if someone had laid a heavy weight on his shoulders. People called Summer crazy, but Ross had liked him from the start. Despite his strange ways, he was a gentle man. And he was still grieving.

Summer looked over at him and smiled. "You're the missing piece in your family puzzle, Ross. Maybe you should think about going back."

Ross didn't even attempt to answer. But for the first time since the fight with his parents, he regretted leaving home.

Walking back to Mary's house, he thought about all that Summer had said. Were his parents grieving for him as Summer was grieving for his wife and daughter? If he walked into the house after all this time away, would they be happy to see him?

His thoughts drifted back to that last night when he and his father had fought over the chicken. He could almost taste his bitterness toward his father, who had called him a liar and struck him for that when he had been telling the truth. If he had thought of it then, he would have insisted that his father go and speak to Fred Myers. The man would have confirmed his story.

For the first time, Ross wondered what had happened to the chicken. He had taken little notice of it after he had laid it on the kitchen floor. All he remembered was that it squawked and fluttered under his feet while he and his father fought.

Thinking about it calmly now, Ross realized that his father would have taken the chicken back to Fred Myers first thing the next morning. Ross could imagine what had happened then. Mr. Myers would have refused to take it back, saying it was payment for the work Ross had done.

Ross breathed a slow sigh. The whole unhappy affair had probably been resolved weeks ago, and all this time he had been burning with resentment toward his parents, wanting to get even with them for sending him away. He had punished them by leaving no clue as to where he had gone. If he went back, he'd have to answer for that. And for stealing money from his brother, too. Staying on the road might be a whole lot easier than going home.

He still couldn't get over how his mother had driven him out. She had turned against him in an instant. He thought of Mary and wondered if she would ever turn against Jimmy with such cold fury. Not in a hundred years!

FIFTEEN

Under swiftly moving black clouds, Ross, Jimmy, and Emily walked along Sweet Spring Road, headed for the brick plant. Ross was going to pick up his last wages before leaving. When Emily learned that Jimmy was going along, she coaxed her mother into letting her go, too. Neither she nor Jimmy had ever been close to a beehive kiln. Today they would get to see one inside and out.

Coming to Summer's house, they found him about to leave. He, too, was walking over to the brick plant to see Mr. Weston. He joined them, explaining that Mr. Weston was interested in buying a couple of goats for his wife.

Just as the five o'clock whistle blew, they turned

into the plant yard. Ross collected his pay, then, leaving Summer talking with Mr. Weston, led Jimmy and Emily down the cinder road beside the beehives.

The first four kilns were sealed, with fires burning in the firepits along the walls. In the kiln where Ross had left his turtle, the bricks had already been removed. The turtle was there on the ledge, burned to a shiny steel gray flecked with bits of black and brown.

"It's beautiful," Emily exclaimed when Ross held it out for her inspection.

"It's like a piece of glass," Jimmy said. "It'll last forever."

"Maybe not that long," Ross replied, "but one of the men told me it would last a hundred years."

"That should be long enough for Hannah," Emily said, smiling.

Jimmy walked to the center of the beehive, cupped his hands around his mouth, and yelled up at the domed roof. "Hello!" Echoes bouncing off the thick brick ceiling made them feel as if they were in a cave.

"I'll bet it gets as hot as a cookstove in here," Emily said.

"Sure does," Ross said. "You can still feel the heat coming out of the bricks."

They wandered out through the arched doorway.

Farther down the cinder road, Ross saw a man hurrying between two beehives.

"Hey, there's Johnny Peale. Come on. I want to show him how my turtle turned out."

They went down the road and cut onto the path between the beehives. Johnny was just ducking out of sight around the corner of a building. Ross had not been in the long wooden building before, but he knew it was the heart of the brick plant. Inside, the raw clay was mixed to the right consistency, then fed into machines and formed into bricks.

"He must have gone in there," Ross said, motioning Jimmy and Emily toward a gray door that was standing ajar.

Entering the building, they paused, waiting for their eyes to adjust to the darkness. Bulky black shapes came into focus, unbaked bricks stacked on carts waiting to be rolled out to the kilns. The dimness and the eerie quiet made Ross feel like shivering. He took a step backward and bumped into Jimmy.

"What is it?" Jimmy whispered.

"I don't know," Ross whispered back. Then suddenly he did know. He smelled smoke. Jimmy and Emily smelled it, too, and in the same instant, the three of them spun back toward the open door.

Just as Ross passed one of the loaded brick carts, someone grabbed his arm, bringing him to an abrupt halt.

"What are you doing in here, Ross?" It was Johnny Peale.

Air rushed out of Ross's lungs as he smiled at his friend. "We were looking for you. But there's something burning in here. We've got to go tell Mr. Weston."

The hold on Ross's arm tightened. "I can't let you do that, Ross."

"What do you mean?" Ross stared at the man.

Without answering, Johnny doubled Ross's arm up behind his back. "I'm sorry you came in here, Ross."

"Ow! You're hurting me." Ross rose up on his toes to ease the pain in his shoulder.

Ignoring Ross's groan, Johnny turned to Jimmy. "Go pull that door shut." He gestured to the door they had just entered. "And bolt it," he added. When Jimmy didn't move, Johnny lowered his voice and took a step toward the boy, dragging Ross with him. "Do it!" he commanded.

The pain in Ross's face, as well as the man's menacing tone, sent Jimmy hurrying to do as he had been ordered. When he returned, Johnny pointed to the other side of the building.

"You and your sister walk over there. I'll be right behind you."

Emily paused as if she intended to argue with him, but Jimmy grabbed her arm and pulled her away. "Come on, Emily. Just do as he says."

They sneaked quick glances over their shoulders at the man behind them. The crackle of flames grew louder, and smoke billowed up into the roof rafters.

Ross's knees were trembling so hard he could barely walk. He pulled against the man's iron grasp. "Where are you taking us?"

"I don't want to hurt any of you, Ross, but you're not going to stop me."

"Stop you! From doing what?"

"Weston fired me today. But he'll be sorry. I'm going to shut down this whole plant." Johnny eased Ross's arm down a little, but didn't release him. "If I can't work, nobody else will either."

"Mr. Weston fired you? But why?"

A shadow darkened Johnny's face. "I took some money from his office. But I had to. My kids were hungry. I couldn't stand to see . . ." His voice trailed away, but then he lifted his chin and fastened flashing eyes on Ross. "I'm going to burn this building to the ground."

Ross's knees finally gave way, and he would

have sagged to the floor if Johnny had not held him up. "But you can't!" he breathed.

"Oh, yes, I can. Burning down a building is easy," Johnny said, pulling Ross over to some burlap sacks piled next to the wall. "Once these sacks are burning, they'll never be able to put the fire out." He handed Ross a matchbox. "Take this and light them." He turned to Jimmy and Emily. "Gather up some of that wood and bring it over here."

"You're going to let us go, aren't you?" Emily asked, even as she bent to pick up a piece of scrap lumber.

"I can't let you go out there and warn them," Johnny said.

"We won't tell anyone you started the fire," Emily said, dropping the wood onto the unlit burlap.

Johnny looked at her for only a moment before turning back to Ross. His wild stare so chilled Ross that his fingers fumbled with the matchbox, and he dropped it. Picking it up, he stared at the familiar blue box. *Blue Moon Café*. Vague images began to take shape in Ross's mind, but before they became clear, Johnny spoke.

"Yes, it was me you saw in Warner Smith's barn, Ross."

Ross still didn't want to believe it. "But why?" he demanded.

Johnny didn't answer, but the look on his face told Ross it was true.

"Why?" Ross asked again. "Why did you . . . ?"

Johnny threw up a hand and glared at Ross. "I worked every day for two weeks digging ditches for Warner Smith, and then he said he didn't have the money to pay me. He promised to pay me later, but my family needed food that day, not later."

The idea of Johnny being the barn burner was almost more than Ross could accept. He had to know for sure. "And the other . . . did you burn the other barns?"

"One belonged to Fred Stills. He ordered my wife off his property when she was picking berries. And he slapped my youngest boy for leaving a gate open." Words tumbled out now, as if Johnny had been waiting for this moment to confess his wrong-doing. "Then last week when I asked Bill Adams if he'd let me put in a patch of potatoes on his farm, he refused. Said he didn't have any garden land." Johnny paused and ran the back of his hand across his forehead. "He owns a hundred and fifteen acres!"

Ross stared at Johnny, not knowing what to say.

"Don't you see, Ross? I couldn't stand to see my

family go hungry. The farmers have plenty, and I don't have enough to keep my kids from hurting."

Suddenly, he seemed to remember where he was and what he intended to do. He waved an arm, signaling Ross to get to work.

In a kind of daze, Ross opened the matchbox and took out a match. Lighting some of the dry grass Johnny had brought for tinder, he coaxed the burlap into flame. It took only a few seconds for the dry wood to catch fire. Ross stood up and faced Johnny.

"Now can we go?"

"No, I need time to get away." The man gestured along the wall. "That way."

There was no use in arguing, but as Ross looked over at Jimmy and Emily, he read a silent message in their eyes. They were asking him what they could do. He shrugged his shoulders in reply. If one of them could get away from Johnny, they could bring help. Ross considered running, but he didn't know if he could find the door. Besides, he was afraid to leave Emily and Jimmy with the man. Johnny was desperate.

The smoke was getting thicker by the minute. They were all coughing, even Johnny. It burned Ross's nose and throat and made his eyes water. "We've got to get out of here," he muttered as much to himself as to the others. Behind him, he saw flames licking up the wall from the burlap and lumber. How long would it take before the roof came crashing down? And where was Johnny taking them? He followed the wall, staggering every time the man gave him a shove from behind.

When Ross saw the door, he rushed toward it. Johnny pushed him aside and fumbled with the rusty bolt. As soon as the door swung open, light and fresh air hit them like cold water thrown in their faces.

Johnny led them out into the cloudy afternoon light, then turned and grabbed hold of Ross and Jimmy. "Over there," he growled, pushing them toward a small wooden shed next to the railroad siding.

Ross guessed it was used for storage, although brush and dead tree limbs were piled against one wall, almost blocking the narrow door.

Johnny shouldered the door open and shoved Jimmy inside, then Ross. "You, too," he said to Emily.

"Don't lock us in here, Johnny," Ross said. "How will we get out?"

"When you hear the men out here fighting the fire, just yell. They'll let you out." He looked at Ross, as if pleading with him to understand. "I'm leaving the valley, and I can't let you send the sheriff after me."

"But what about your family?" Ross blurted out as the door started to close.

Johnny stopped and stared at him. He shook his head. "I'm no good to them anymore. They'll be better off without me." Then he pushed the door shut.

There was the paralyzing sound of a bolt sliding into place, then silence. Ross reached out and pressed against the wooden door, but it didn't give an inch. He waited for his eyes to get used to the darkness. If there was a window, they might be able to crawl out, but there was no light coming in except what filtered through cracks between the boards. A damp, earthy odor arose from the dirt floor.

Jimmy's unsteady voice came out of the gloom. "It sure is dark in here."

"We won't be in here long," Ross said. "They'll see the smoke pretty soon."

"Do you think . . ." Emily began, then stopped and cleared her throat. "Do you think there are any snakes in here?"

Ross smiled, and the smile widened when he heard Jimmy suck in a loud breath. "I doubt it," Ross said. "Snakes get out in the sun during the day. Their favorite spot is a sunny back porch."

Emily made a hissing noise, but Ross knew she was smiling, too.

"Do you suppose they've seen the smoke yet?" Jimmy asked.

"If they haven't, they'd better wake up," Emily told him. "Listen. The fire is roaring."

Amid the roar were crackling noises and an occasional thud as a burned beam gave way. It seemed to Ross that he could feel the heat, even through the walls of the shed.

They took turns peering out at the deserted yard through an inch-wide crack in the door. After a while, they sank down on the cool floor to wait.

Ross thought of Johnny Peale hurrying along some back road, trying to get out of the valley before someone connected him with the fire. Ross remembered when he had been in the same predicament. But he had been innocent, and Johnny was guilty.

If they caught Johnny, he would surely go to jail. Even if he got out of the valley and evaded the law, Ross knew the man was leaving behind the only thing that really mattered to him, his family.

Suddenly, they heard men's voices, excited, shouting. The three of them jumped up and began pounding on the shed door.

"Help! Over here! We're in the shed by the tracks. Help!"

They screamed until they were out of breath,

then paused, listening for approaching footsteps. The roar of the fire and the clamoring voices went on as before. Nobody came to open the door.

"They can't hear us," Ross said. "We'll just have to wait until the fire dies down."

Emily and Jimmy took turns shouting, while Ross leaned against the wall and listened to the frantic firefighters, so close and yet so far. He could still taste the smoke, or maybe it had worked its way through the cracks into the shed. A popping noise caught his attention, not distant as they had heard before, but much closer. He pushed away from the wall and tilted his head, trying to figure out where it was coming from and what it could be.

"Quiet!" he called out, cutting off Jimmy's shout. "Listen." They stood motionless, hardly breathing. Smoke scorched Ross's throat as he drew in a breath. Then his heart seemed to stop. He could see red through the cracks in the wall. Fire! And it was just outside the shed.

When he laid his hand on the wall, the wood felt warm to his touch. Then he remembered the pile of dried brush near the shed door. He knew in an instant what had happened. Sparks from the burning building had floated through the air and set the brush afire. It wouldn't be long before the shed would be burning, too. The men fighting the fire probably would not notice such a small fire, and even if they did, they would let it burn. The big building was more important. Besides, they didn't know there was anyone in the shed.

Ross pushed again on the bolted door, even though he knew it was hopeless. Stomach fluttering and legs trembling, he leaned against the wall for support. There was no way out.

He and Emily and Jimmy stood there in the darkness, unable to speak. There was nothing to say anyway. They were trapped—and they knew it.

SIXTEEN

Ross sagged down on the floor where the smoke was not quite so thick. In the suffocating darkness, he thought of home. It seemed hazy and far away, like a land he had visited once long ago. But the faces were clear in his mind. He shook his head. He could not think of them, not now when they were unreachable.

Emily pounded on the door and shouted. "Help! The building's on fire! Let us out!" It was no use. They couldn't hear her. The men's voices grew fainter as the fire beside the shed intensified.

Panic boiled in Ross. A way out . . . a way out! Maybe they could dig a hole under the wall. He scooted over and clawed at the dirt where the shed boards touched the ground. But the foundation stones had been buried deep in the earth, and there was no hope of digging under them. He stood up, his mind whirling.

Maybe if all three of them pushed on the door, the bolt would give way. He called Jimmy and Emily to help him. Hands flattened against the hot boards, they pushed with all their strength, but the door remained solidly in place. It was hopeless, Ross thought, like trying to move a barn-size boulder.

The three of them paced around the small space like animals in a cage. They could see blue flames curling between the cracks around the door. Fire whispered along the roof. Heat kept building inside the shed, an intense, dry heat that seemed to suck away the air. There was no relief from the choking smoke.

When Ross heard himself gasping for air, he felt a sudden hot anger. He wasn't going to die in here! There had to be a way out, a loose board, a rotten timber.

He moved along the wall, running his hands carefully over the splintery boards. Hardly any light came through the tightly nailed siding. If only he could see! Turning the corner, he fingered a piece of wood protruding slightly from the wall. There was something there. His heart jumped as his fingers touched the cool pane of glass. A window! But why was there no light? It must be boarded up on the outside. Well, first they would break the glass, then they would work at loosening the boards.

Emily appeared beside Ross. "What are you doing?"

"There's a window here. We have to break it. Try to find a rock or a piece of wood, anything hard."

Jimmy and Emily crawled across the floor, feeling inch by inch, while Ross continued his examination of the walls. Their frantic search produced nothing. The smoke and heat were almost unbearable now. Their voices were raw, and every breath brought pain. They didn't have much time.

"Kick it with your foot," Jimmy croaked.

The window was too far above Ross. "I can't reach it," he said. "And there's nothing to stand on."

"Your shoe," Emily cried weakly. "Use your shoe to break it."

Ross jerked off a shoe and felt for the windowpane. "Stand back," he warned them.

Covering his face with his left arm, he swung

at the glass. Nothing happened. He struck again, but still it did not break. After more than a dozen tries, he gave up. His leather shoe was no match for the thick windowpane. Slipping his shoe back on, he swiped at his watering eyes. The door and the whole wall were ablaze now, and flames crept along the ceiling toward them. Even if the men came to save them, escape through the door was impossible now. Their only hope was the window.

Staring at the approaching fire, Ross slid his hands into his pockets. There was only one thing to do: try to break the glass with his fist. He would get cut, he knew, but . . . Suddenly, his fingers closed around the baked clay turtle. He had forgotten the heavy object was in his pocket until he touched it. Baked clay was hard enough to shatter any glass!

He yanked it out of his pocket, then shouted, "Watch out!" and swung hard. Glass exploded in a shower of stinging shards. Hardly feeling the cuts on his hands and arms, Ross scraped away the broken glass. Then he turned to Jimmy and Emily.

"I can't reach the boards. You'll have to boost me up."

Clasping each other's wrists, Jimmy and

Emily created a shelf for Ross to step on. Slowly they lifted him up. He scrambled onto the window's narrow ledge, then began pounding on the outer boards. It took several blows before a board broke away from the nails holding it. The sudden burst of light blinded Ross.

"Hurry!" Jimmy shouted, then doubled over in a fit of coughing.

Ross took a deep breath and put all his strength into knocking out the remaining boards. When he was unable to loosen any more with his hands, he used his feet. After kicking away the last board, he peered back into the smoky shed. Emily stood looking up, her eyes watering, her cheeks as red as the fire closing in. Jimmy was on his knees, coughing.

"Hurry!" Ross said, reaching a hand down to Emily.

Instead of taking his hand, she shook her head. "Jimmy first," she shouted.

"This is no time to argue," Ross shouted back.

But Emily was not listening. She knelt by her brother, put an arm around his waist, and pulled him to his feet. Then, interlacing her fingers, palms up, she ordered him to start climbing. With Emily lifting and Ross pulling, they managed to get Jimmy up to the open window.

Breathing in clean air, he quickly revived and scrambled outside.

When Ross reached down for Emily, he saw her kneeling beside the wall. Maybe she was too weak now to climb out. Just as he was thinking he would have to go back into the shed to help her, she stood up. With a flashing grin, she reached up and took his hands. Moments later, she was through the window and on the ground. Ross dropped down beside her.

The three of them backed away to a safe distance, then watched in silence as flames enveloped the shed.

"Jimmy, your arm!" Emily burst out. A long cut oozed blood, running down her brother's arm and dripping off the ends of his fingers.

Just then, they saw Summer hurrying toward them. The little man stared from one to the other without saying a word. Then he noticed Jimmy's arm. "Come along, Jimmy. Mr. Weston has a first-aid kit in his office."

They were almost to the office door when Calvin appeared beside them. "Thought maybe I could help," he said. "I've had plenty of practice tending cuts and bruises around here. This one doesn't look too bad."

He motioned Jimmy into a chair, then went

over and took down a white tin box from a shelf. Setting to work, he washed out the wound with a clear liquid that made Jimmy yelp, then wrapped the arm in a tight bandage. "It'll be fine in a few days," he said. "Just keep it clean."

While Calvin was treating Jimmy, Ross told Summer what had happened. The man listened, his frown deepening as Johnny Peale's part in the story came out.

"You'll have to explain it all to the sheriff," Summer said.

Ross agreed, but for some reason he felt guilty, as if he were forced to betray a friend.

The big building was a flaming mountain now. There was no hope of bringing the fire under control, so the men just stood and watched it burn. A final section of the roof caved in, sending out a tidal wave of heat and smoke and ashes. Some of the men hurried forward to contain the fire, shoveling scraps of burning debris back toward the smoldering ruins.

There were men still arriving, men who had left for home but returned when they saw the giant smoke cloud in the sky. Though the fire would continue to smolder far into the night, there was no more danger of its spreading.

The sheriff questioned Ross, Jimmy, and

Emily. After he had heard the whole story, he told them they could go home. Summer went with them, describing his panic when he couldn't locate them anywhere at the plant.

"Finding you all safe was like seeing a rainbow after a storm," he finished, with his missing-tooth grin.

As they walked toward the plant gate, a deputy's car turned into the yard. Before the car came to a stop, the passenger door flew open and Mary jumped out. She paused for a few seconds to stare from Jimmy to Emily to Ross. Then she rushed forward, swooping all three of them into a fierce embrace. Her crooning words were meaningless, unintelligible, but to Ross they were like beautiful music. He just closed his eyes and melted into her love.

SEVENTEEN

Light filtering through the bedroom curtains gave the flowered wallpaper a soft yellow tint. Beneath the faded quilt, Ross stretched, hesitant to let this day begin. He had been hoping for weeks to get out of Laurel Valley, but now that he was leaving, he did not want to go.

He thought of how it had been on the road, how it would be again: long days of walking, days of worrying where his next meal was coming from and where he would spend the night. He still would have no destination, no place where he could stop and say, "I'm home."

Worst of all was having to leave Mary and the others. He remembered Mary's desperate fear at the brick plant when she had gathered the three of them into her arms. She had embraced him as if he were one of her own. Of all her stumbling words of relief and joy, one sentence lingered in Ross's mind like a haunting tune. She had said over and over, "I'd do anything to keep you from being hurt."

Those comforting words reminded Ross of his mother. She would have been just as frightened, just as fiercely protective.

He sat up in bed. His mother's face appeared before him as if she were right there in the room, saying once again, "Get out of my sight." But suddenly, the words took on new meaning. Like the sun coming from behind a cloud, he realized he had been wrong about everything.

"She did it on purpose," he murmured, not even knowing he spoke out loud. There had been no cruelty in his mother's words. Upset and shocked by what was happening between Ross and his father, she had known that the only way of keeping him safe for that moment, for that night, was to force him out of the house. So she had deliberately driven him away, using harsh words like a slashing weapon to make him go.

Ross balled his fists into his eyes. All these weeks he had been thinking his mother hated him, wanted him gone. Instead, she had pretended to be angry simply to protect him.

An image of Johnny Peale stole into his mind. The man had tried to protect his children, too. But when he thought that people were keeping him from getting food for his family, he had struck out at them, setting fires, wanting them to hurt as he was hurting. All Ross could recall of his last glimpse of Johnny was the sadness in the man's face, and the despair. Ross wondered if he had gotten out of the valley. If he had, maybe he would be able to get a job somewhere and send money back to his family.

In some strange way, the picture of Johnny Peale comforted him. It helped him to understand how hard it was to take care of a family. If he ever went home again, he might still have to deal with his father's anger, but at least now he understood it.

As Ross sat there, he gradually became aware of the sounds in the kitchen. Everyone must be up but him. He climbed out of bed and jerked on his clothes.

When he stepped into the kitchen, they looked at him with wary, shifting glances. He washed his hands and face, wondering why they were so quiet. Even when he sat down at the table, no one said a word.

Then he saw the burned clay turtle next to his plate. His questioning gaze flashed to Emily.

She grinned. "I found it on the floor just before I climbed out of the shed."

Ross picked it up and studied it for a moment, then handed it to Hannah. "I made this for you. It's a little scratched up, but it'll still last a while."

"Thank you, Ross Cooper," she said, cradling the turtle in her two small hands. Then she smiled at him and added, "We had a meeting, and we all voted yes."

What was she talking about? Ross looked around at the others. Jimmy shrugged his shoulders and grinned, and Emily's eyes glowed with a secretive light. Mary looked quite serious. She straightened her shoulders and held Ross with her level gaze.

"We've talked things over." She paused, as if she had run short of air. Then she actually gulped in a big breath. "We'd like you to stay here and live with us."

Ross stared at her. What he'd been hoping for had finally happened. He could think of plenty of reasons for staying. Mary still needed help, at least until her husband came home. There was the house and the garden, and those three chicks would have to be carefully guarded. Summer might need his help again with his fences or some other project. And he and Jimmy hadn't been back yet to take a ride on Bill Adams's mare.

There might even be work at the brick factory. He recalled Mr. Weston scoffing at Johnny Peale's threat to shut down the plant.

"He hasn't put us out of business," Mr. Weston had said, watching the building burn. "We'll just form the bricks in wooden molds until we can get new brick-making machines."

If he went back to work at the plant, Ross thought, he could make some more clay animals. Emily might like a baby rabbit. He gazed across the table at Mary. At a time when he needed a place to stay, she had taken him in. He could never repay her for that, and for believing in him when he told the story of the burning barn. Now she was offering him a permanent home. It was like having an incredible dream come true.

Swallowing to get rid of the burning in his throat, Ross met her hopeful, waiting gaze. Then slowly he shook his head, not knowing until that very moment what an important decision he had already made.

The kitchen grew so still that Ross could hear his own heart beating. Jimmy slammed his fist into his hand.

"I was planning on—"

Hannah interrupted him with a groan. "Don't go, Ross Cooper."

Emily laid an arm around her sister's shoulders, and her shining eyes, meeting Ross's, seemed to say the same thing.

Mary leaned forward in her chair. "I hate to think of you going back on the road, Ross. You need three meals a day and a place to sleep at night."

"I know," Ross said, letting a smile spread across his face. "I've decided to take your advice. I'm going home."

"Oh, Ross." Tears glistened in Mary's eyes as she got up from her chair and came around the table. She bent over and laid her cheek on top of his head. "I understand. But you'll always have a home here. Remember that."

Ross smiled at the others around the table, feeling light and airy, like a feather on a breeze. He was thankful that they began talking, and he ducked his head and swallowed hard before he took his first bite of food.

After breakfast, he went upstairs and packed everything into his knapsack. Before leaving the room, he took out two dollar bills and laid them on the bed. Mary would need the money more than he would.

They were all waiting for him in the kitchen, shuffling from place to place, casting sidelong glances at him. Mary came up and held out her hand. In her palm lay a penny and a piece of paper.

"Ross, I want you to send us a postcard when you get home. I've written down our address."

When he hesitated, Mary went on. "Please, Ross. We want to know you made it home safely."

He reached out and took only the paper. "I have money," he said. "I'll let you know when I'm home. It may take a week, unless I'm awfully lucky hitching rides."

Mary picked up a bundle from the table. "I've packed you a little lunch."

Ross took it and stashed it in his knapsack, dreading to face her for the last time. "Thank you, for everything."

"We were glad to have you here, Ross. Thank you for all the work you did." She reached out and hugged him, squeezing him so tightly she made him grunt.

Hannah came and hugged him, too, though she couldn't reach any higher than his waist. Ross and Jimmy grinned at each other.

"Watch out for Mr. Morris's shotgun," Ross said.

"Stay out of burning barns," came Jimmy's quick reply.

When Ross's gaze swung to Emily, she took a step

forward and held out her hand. In it was Ross's shirt, the one the goat had chewed on and torn.

"I patched it," she said, then with a trace of laughter in her voice added, "that's women's work."

Ross grinned at her and slipped the shirt into his knapsack. Even though he knew he was just dawdling, he took his time snugging his hat on his head, then settling the knapsack over his shoulder. Pushing through the screen door, he paused to gaze at the rich green landscape. He would remember these hills. When he went down the steps, Jimmy was close behind.

"I reckon I'll walk along with you to the main road."

They had taken only a few steps when Hannah came running alongside. "I'm going, too," she said. She slipped her hand into Ross's and looked up at him. "Promise you'll come back, Ross Cooper."

"I promise," he said without a moment's hesitation. If he did not make it this year before school started, he would come next summer, for sure.

They started on but had not gone far when they heard running footsteps behind them. "I guess I'll walk along, too," Emily said, flashing Ross an impish smile.

They were almost out of the yard when Mary shouted from the porch, "Wait for me."

Together, the five of them strolled down the valley. Ross deliberately walked at a slow pace, and everyone else matched their steps to his. He need not hurry, he told himself. A few minutes here in Laurel Valley was not going to make any difference in a trip that would take him several days. Later, when he was on the road, when he was alone, he would let his thoughts turn toward home.

About the Author

Patricia Willis has written several well-received historical novels. Her most recent book, *Danger Along the Ohio*, received the Spur Award for Best Western Juvenile Fiction and was described by *Kirkus Reviews* as "a rousing adventure" and by the *School Library Journal* as having "the suspense of a page-turner, the danger level of a thriller, and the fascination of a survival story." Ms. Willis lives in North Canton, Ohio.